Cookied

A Little-Pinch-of-Murder Cozy Mystery

Miranda Rose Barker

Creative Bookworm Press

This is a work of fiction. Names, characters, places, and incidents are either products of the author's imagination or are used fictitiously. Any similarity to actual events, organizations, locales or persons, living or dead, is entirely coincidental.

Copyright © 2023 by Miranda Rose Barker

All rights reserved.

No portion of this book may be reproduced in any form without written permission from the publisher or author, except as permitted by U.S. copyright law.

www.MirandaRoseBarker.com

Like Miranda Rose's Facebook Page at
https://www.facebook.com/mirandarosebarker

A Creative Bookworm Press Publication

Published by Creative Bookworm LLC, Tucson, Arizona

https://www.CreativeBookworm.com

Claim Your FREE Gift

Dear Mystery Story Fan,

Sign up for my newsletter to get a free book, updates, and new book announcements!

Don't miss out on my next new book releases as soon as they are available in my cozy mysteries, dog lovers' rescue romances, and other series.

Plus, I'll send you information on my latest plans for upcoming book projects, along with other offers for free reads.

Just click below to sign up, and we'll see you on the other side...

Click Here to Claim Your Free Book & My Newsletter Updates

Or Visit This Link

https://mirandarosebarker.com/cozy-mystery-offer

Book Series by This Author

Visit https://mirandarosebarker.com/mrbauthorpage
The Dog Lovers' Rescue Romance Series
The Very Human Dog Lover Story Series
The Dogs Are Family Too Series
The Tansy & Hank Pet Psychic Cozy Mystery Series
The Sycamore Grove Paranormal Cozy Mystery Series
The Near-To-Home Mystery Series
The Sweets of Saltcaster Cozy Mystery Series
The Sweets of Snowkeep Cozy Mystery Series
The Little-Pinch-of-Murder Cozy Mystery Series

Other Dog Lover Books Published by Creative Bookworm Press:

Chew on Things, It Helps You Think: Words of Wisdom from a Worried Canine

Chew on Things Workbook for Fellow Worriers

Contents

1. Chapter One — 1
2. Chapter Two — 6
3. Chapter Three — 11
4. Chapter Four — 16
5. Chapter Five — 24
6. Chapter Six — 30
7. Chapter Seven — 35
8. Chapter Eight — 42
9. Chapter Nine — 49
10. Chapter Ten — 53
11. Chapter Eleven — 56
12. Chapter Twelve — 59
13. Chapter Thirteen — 65
14. Chapter Fourteen — 69
15. Chapter Fifteen — 74
16. Chapter Sixteen — 78
17. Chapter Seventeen — 83

18.	Chapter Eighteen	88
19.	Chapter Nineteen	95
20.	Chapter Twenty	102
	About the Author	107
	Remember To Claim Your Free Gift	109
	Mysteries by the Author	111

Chapter One

It was finally time. After years of planning and yearning and scrimping and saving, I was only one week away from the grand opening of my bakery: *Pyrus's Pastries*. It was crazy that I was able to say that. *My* bakery. A place that I owned and built and cultivated myself. It was my vision, and it was days away from being open.

It was named after my best friend and cheerleader, Pyrus. She'd been with me through thick and thin, a constant in my life. I loved her deeply, and she loved me.

Pyrus was currently pitter-pattering around my feet while I sipped on my morning coffee. She really was the cutest. If I wasn't careful, she'd be the most spoiled dog in the world. Sometimes, all it took was one look, and I was ready to give her anything she asked for.

As I watched her stroll around my legs, rubbing her body against me, I was able to deduce what she wanted. She wanted a little attention. A little love. I gave her a quick pet and then threw her one of her favorites, some homemade peanut butter dog treats I planned on stocking at the bakery. She chomped on the dog treat, enjoying it to the fullest.

"Are you ready, Pyrus?" She looked up at me with what I swore was a look of determination. Even though Pyrus was a dog, I felt like she was offering me a little support. She was a dog, so her abilities were limited, but her go-tos were coming to me to cuddle, and she really did get this look on her face. It was hard to describe without sounding like a crazy dog mom, but I swore it was real.

Pyrus was always there for me when I needed her, and it wasn't just because I was her owner. Our bond went deeper than that. It was why we were able to give each other such poignant comfort.

And I needed a lot of that these days. It had been quite the struggle getting everything ready for the grand opening. What could go wrong went wrong.

Constantly.

Equipment that didn't work. Health inspectors pushing back appointments. Pipes bursting. A fire.

A freaking fire!

God, it was absolutely horrifying. Thankfully, no one was in the bakery when it went up, and the firefighters were able to get there before the whole thing went up in flames. Because of that there wasn't too much damage, but I almost gave up. The smoke damage was pretty extensive and was going to take a bit of elbow grease to address. At that point, I was beginning to believe that it just wasn't meant to be.

But then I saw Pyrus's wet eyes, and she whimpered a little, her little snout booping against me. Even without words, I knew exactly what she was trying to tell me. I was fine with disappointing myself, but I could not disappoint my dog.

Baking was a passion that had followed me all through life. I used to bake with my mother all the time. It was just the two of us, and she taught me everything she knew. Eventually, I was able to teach her a thing or two. We had always spoken about opening a bakery together, but she died before our dream was realized.

Pyrus came to me not too long after my mom's death. I'd never owned a dog or thought about owning one, but back when I had a roommate, she had impulsively rescued a dog and then suddenly got a job in the Netherlands. I suspected she'd met a man and just didn't want to admit it. Either way, I found myself with this dog. Early days were testy, but soon enough Pyrus and I bonded. Maybe it was a mutual feeling of abandonment, but ever since, we were inseparable.

I sometimes wondered if she was sent to help me get through those tough days.

And we'd made it through. We were just one week away from running our own bakery. Through Pyrus, a lot had proven to be possible, and I was hoping I'd have some of her good juju to get me through this upcoming interview.

I'd been looking for an assistant even before I'd bought this building. Before I went down the owning a bakery route, I was making cookies and cakes in my household kitchen. At first, I would only do orders I could personally deliver myself but eventually expanded to shipping orders out. I kept the radius small to avoid overwhelming myself, but I did hope that if things really picked up, I could deliver to more and more people.

I'd need help to do that though. The operation was already pretty stressful, and I didn't want to overextend myself to the point of failure.

But it'd been hard finding just the right person. For whatever reason, Park Perdsor, Rhode Island just wasn't home to a community of baking professionals. And if I did manage to find someone halfway decent, they were always just passing through.

The difficulties of being a local in a tourist trap...

But I was trying to stay positive about today's applicant. Callie Pierson. We'd spoken on the phone briefly, but this was our first in-person meeting. She sounded really sweet on the phone, and we had a really great conversation. Her resume showed a lack of experience, but I was always open to teaching…if the person was the right fit.

I kneeled down and scratched Pyrus under her chin.

"I hope you like her, girl." Pyrus ignored me and licked the dog treat remnants on my fingers. Once she was good and done, I drank the rest of my coffee and got the two of us ready to head to the bakery for Callie's interview.

"You're the one that I want, the one that I really really want!"

"Woof, woof, woof!"

"Honey!"

Pyrus and I sang our little hearts out as I drove us over to the bakery. I had queued up my movie musical playlist for the short drive over. *Grease* was always a big hit with Pyrus. Something about Olivia Newton John's voice made her want to sing along. *Xanadu* was a close second.

The song wasn't over when we pulled into the parking lot, so I let it finish before turning off the car. Pyrus and I were feeling more invigorated and ready for the day already. I kept repeating affirmations to myself, and I was actually starting to believe them.

The grand opening will go well.

I'm going to find a killer assistant.

My business will succeed.

This is my time. My time to shine.

I'd waited long enough. Gone through enough strife and hardship, and I'd come out on the other side of it. It was time to reap some of the benefits of all that struggle.

I took Pyrus to the outdoor seating area behind the bakery, so I could bake cookies in the kitchen. It was our signature recipe, inspired by my dog's love of pears. It was actually where I got her name from. Originally, my old roommate called her Pearl, but that felt a little too... precious for the kind of dog Pyrus was. And when I learned she loved pears, I looked up the different names for them and settled on Pyrus. I felt like it just fit.

I wanted to bake some of my pear cookies (with and without chocolate chips) for Callie before she got here. It wasn't a requirement to like the food made here, but it'd be nice. And I thought it'd be a good idea to do the baking of it at the bakery.

Baking was always extremely cathartic for me, and I wanted to bring that good juju into the space.

I needed all the good juju I could get.

I got to work measuring and pouring and mixing. I liked to use fresh pears as opposed to flavoring or a concentrate, because *I* believed it made the cookie feel lighter. It meant juicing my own pears, which was *a lot* of work, but the end product was worth it. These were absolutely perfect warm, gooey, tasty pear and chocolate chip cookies. Of course, I also had a dog-friendly version, sans chocolate, so everyone could get in on the fun.

I took Pyrus's treat out to her before plating the cookies I had made for Callie. I still had a couple hours before she'd arrive, so I played with Pyrus a little bit and answered some emails. Though the cookies had helped calm me down some, it was apparent I hadn't quite let go of all my anxieties. Achieving total calm was probably an impossible mission. Firstly, I was a naturally nervous person, but it also didn't help that my life liked to keep things interesting.

I just hoped Callie wouldn't pick up on my nervous energy and think I was some kind of nut.

Chapter Two

"Hello?"

Pyrus and I both looked up when we heard an unfamiliar voice calling from the front of the store. We put down what we were doing—I was answering emails while Pyrus was very focused on a chew toy—and headed to see who it could be.

I peeked my head around the corner and saw a young woman standing in the bakery.

"Hi." She gave me a tentative smile and walked up to the counter. She was about my height with her brunette hair tied up in a ponytail.

"I'm Callie Pierson. I have an interview."

Of course! Hearing her name, I jumped into action.

"Callie! Hi!" I glanced at the clock on the wall and heard a nervous chuckle.

"I'm a little early. Sorry. I thought the drive would take a lot longer, but I grossly miscalculated, and so here I am." She shrugged. I knew she wasn't local to Park Perdsor, and that coupled with the anxiety of a job interview. I fully understood her desire to be *very* on time.

"Oh my goodness, don't even worry about it." I was just so happy to see her. It had only been a minute, but I already felt good about Callie. I wasn't sure what it was, but something inside of me was getting excited.

"Why don't we head to the back. There's somewhere we can sit outside if you don't mind."

"Sure." She smiled and followed me and Pyrus as we led her outside.

Pyrus went back to her chew toy while Callie and I sat down. Callie glanced over at Pyrus a few times, so I could tell she was interested in her. So, I decided to introduce them.

"Callie, this is Pyrus. Pyrus, Callie."

"Oh, like in *Pyrus's Pastries*," she noticed.

"Yep, she's our mascot, my little helper, and my best friend." Pyrus turned her head and looked at us. It was probably because she heard her name, but I liked to think that she knew this was an important introduction.

"Can I pet her?"

"Of course! She's really friendly." Callie knelt in front of Pyrus and offered a hand for her to sniff. It didn't take long for the two of them to get comfortable with one another. While Callie petted her, she turned to me.

"What kind of dog is she?"

"A terrier mix, probably with border terrier and something else."

"She's so beautiful," Callie cooed while scratching Pyrus's tummy. After a couple minutes of good pets, Callie finished up and rejoined me at the table. Pyrus went back to her chew toy, her little tail wagging.

"So, before we start, I just wanted to give you a taste of what this bakery has to offer." I pulled out the plate of cookies I had made for her, setting them down between us. "Here at *Pyrus's Pastries*, I hope to offer a wide array of sweet treats, but these cookies are really what started the whole thing. They are pear and chocolate chip."

Callie took one from the plate before taking a small bite. She smiled as she swallowed.

"They're really good," she said before going in for a bigger chunk. It always gave me a warm feeling watching people enjoy the food I made.

"So, tell me a little about yourself. Your baking experience."

"Oh, well..." Callie covered her mouth while she finished chewing her cookie. Once she was finished, she continued. "I've only really baked at home. Cookies and cakes and stuff. Um..." Callie bit her lip as her face revealed she was deep in thought. "Sorry," she apologized sheepishly. "I'm never good at answering those "tell me about you" questions. I feel like my mind goes blank."

"It is pretty vague, isn't it?" I moved onto my next question, wanting to keep the conversation flowing. "What's your favorite thing to bake?"

"I like making pies. I usually make them around the holidays. I also make lemon bars." Callie had a habit of looking away while she answered my questions. I wondered if helped her think. I didn't find it unpleasant, just an observation I... observed.

My mother used to say I was too observant. It made sense for someone whose head was often in the cloud. She'd always be surprised by the conclusions I was able to come to, but it all felt so natural to me because it was just things I was seeing.

Over time, I did learn that I didn't have to verbalize everything, but I still kept making my observations. I almost couldn't help it. It came second nature to me.

"Why Park Perdsor?" While we got the usual summer and holiday boosts, it was rare to see an outsider come to stay during the off-season. As far as I knew, Callie didn't have any connection to my small Rhode Island town. We rarely got newcomers, and when we spoke on the phone, she told me she was moving to town shortly.

"Well, my family came here over the summer a couple times when I was a kid. It just stuck in my mind, and recently, I felt something bringing me back here." Callie's face became very thoughtful, and it felt like a moment of vulnerability. She didn't offer any more of an explanation, and given that we had just met, it didn't feel like it was my place to pry.

But I could understand that deep feeling of needing to *do* something. As if you were being guided by forces beyond your understanding.

"Well, I hope we live up to the sunny memories of your youth!"

Callie broke out of her small reverie and smiled with relief. "It's been lovely so far. I visited the old lighthouse on my first day here. I'd seen it before, but it had been years."

Like many coastal towns, Park Perdsor had its own historic lighthouse. I liked to say we had a few extra somethings that made us the more attractive destination, but people really seemed to like lighthouses. I understood it to a certain degree, but having been around them all my life, I never found myself getting as excited as the different tourists who visited our town.

Still, I liked to visit it from time to time. The cliffside it stood on had a beautiful view of the coast. It was a nice spot to go on a picnic or just go to sit and think.

"I'm glad you are enjoying it so far. Do you plan on being around for a while?"

"I'd like to hang around for a bit. As long as Park Perdsor will have me?" She shrugged.

"Oh, I think the people around here will like you. You're so sweet, you'll fit right in!"

"Thanks."

I leaned back in my chair and thought about what it would be like to have Callie working with me in the bakery. She was on the shy side, but I could tell she had a passion inside of her. I wasn't sure if that passion was for baking, but it sounded like she would work hard and be fun to have around. Plus, it would be nice to teach what I knew to someone else.

So many people thrived on the secrecy of their trade, but I believed that just kept people from wanting to try different things out. If someone wanted to learn some baking techniques or the ingredients I used? Well, I was more than happy to share.

We talked for a little bit longer. I told Callie about my vision for the bakery, how I got my start. The conversation just flowed. She was easy to talk to, and as our interview went on, it felt less like a formal "thing" and more like two friends catching up. I felt confident that the two of us would mesh really well together.

"Callie, you've been an absolute delight to talk to, and I want to offer you the job. Right here, right now."

"Really?"

"You can start as early as tomorrow. I will teach you everything you need to know. What do you say to becoming a baker here at *Pyrus's Pastries*?"

"Yes! I would love to work with you, and I can totally start tomorrow."

I got down to business and gave Callie some forms she would need to fill out before she could start. "Just bring these with you tomorrow morning, and we can get you started in the kitchen!"

Callie looked down at everything I had given her. "Okay, I'll work on these tonight and bring them with me tomorrow. Is there anything else?"

"I've got some aprons, but I'd say wear some clothes you don't mind getting a little flour on." Callie nodded, and we said goodbye.

Everything was finally starting to line up, and I couldn't be happier. I was so close to having an up and running bakery!

Chapter Three

I woke up the next morning, and everything was lighter and brighter. Sure, it was still dark when I pulled myself out of bed, but I was feeling so happy that I didn't even need the sun to brighten my day.

After getting myself all cleaned up in the morning, I took Pyrus out for her morning walk.

"What should I show Callie today? I guess I should find out what she already knows. Maybe we could bake something together? I should probably show her our order system…" I continued throwing different ideas at Pyrus, waiting to see if any of them really piqued her interest. She was more enamored with the sidewalk smells than coming up with an onboarding plan. I couldn't blame her.

Pyrus's morning walk was similar to her having her first cup of coffee in the morning. Without that walk, she was kind of out of it. She just wasn't really totally tuned in. We differed in this regard. Sometimes, I needed that extra boost, but some mornings, I subsisted on pure energy.

And that was one of those mornings. I was just so excited that things with my bakery were on the right track.

Once Pyrus finished with her business, we headed back home to have breakfast. I added some rotisserie chicken pieces to her kibble because I wanted us both to have an extra hearty breakfast. I made myself a bowl of oatmeal, giving it all the fixings. Fresh fruit, cinnamon, a little honey.

With our bellies full and our heads held high, Pyrus and I headed to the storefront. Callie was already waiting for us when we pulled up. I made a mental note to myself to get her a key. If being early was her thing, I wouldn't want to make her wait for me every morning.

As I parked the car, I heard the tell-tale sign of a little pup who needed to pee.

"I knew you didn't pee enough this morning," I chastised Pyrus. She usually peed three times during our walk, but she only went once this morning. I gave her an extra ten minutes of walking, but Pyrus seemed done, and I couldn't *force* her to pee. Plus, if I waited too long, we'd end up being late, so I ended the walk.

But it would appear that I had incorrectly assessed the situation.

I held onto Pyrus's leash, and we both got out of the car. There was enough slack, so she could run into the grass to pee. While Pyrus did her business, I beckoned Callie over and handed her the keys.

"I'm going to finish up with her out here. Why don't you head to the kitchen, I'll be in in a few minutes." Handoff complete, I walked closer to Pyrus. Callie unlocked the door and gave me a little wave before heading inside.

I thought going on a mini-walk before heading inside would be a good idea, just in case she needed more than one quick pee to empty her bladder. It would also give Callie a chance to get settled, look around without having to worry about me hovering over her shoulder. Not that I would, but she might have been feeling a little nervous, given that it was her first day.

Pyrus guided our walk, and I was enjoying the warm sunlight when suddenly—

CRASH

"AHHHHHHH!"

The most distressed scream I have ever heard cut through the air. Immediately, I could tell it was coming from the bakery, which meant it was Callie. I raced inside with Pyrus to see what was wrong.

"Callie! Callie!" I called her name. I didn't see her in the front which meant she had to have gone to the back. To the kitchen probably.

Please let everything be okay...

Abandoning all thoughts of cleanliness or health regulations, I let Pyrus follow me into the kitchen. I first saw Callie standing still, her face in shock. As I approached her, I followed her eyeline to see a man lying on the ground.

"Oh my god!" The sight of him caused me to jump a little. Of all the ways I expected my day to go, this was maybe the least expected.

"He's dead!" Callie gasped. I wasn't sure what to think or what to do at first. I just stared at this man, whom I did not know, lying dead in my kitchen. He didn't look that much older than me. I'd seen dead bodies before. I was there with my mom when she died, but this was very different.

"Did you check?" I asked Callie.

"What?" She sharply turned her head towards me. She wiped the tears away from her cheeks. "What do you mean?"

"If he's really dead. Did you check if he's really dead?"

"I—No." Callie shook her head. "I haven't gotten close." I didn't blame her. It wasn't instinctual to approach a dead person.

I handed Pyrus's leash to Callie, not wanting her to get too close. She'd been calm so far, but I had no frame of reference for how my dog would react to being up close to a corpse.

I took a deep breath and tentatively approached the body. I knelt in front of him. Being this close, I did not have much hope that this man was alive.

The pallor of his skin and the bruise on the side of his head did not look good. He wasn't moving at all. I didn't see any chest movements to indicate that he was possibly breathing.

I picked up his wrist anyway. His skin was so cold. I'd never touched a dead body like this before. When my mother died, I had been in the hospital with her, so she wasn't long dead. But this guy, he had been dead for a while. There was no warmth left in him. It was strange feeling such a lack of heat in someone's limbs.

I placed my fingers over his wrist like I had been taught to do and waited a few moments to see if there was any pulse. There was nothing. I counted out the seconds. The moment I reached the recommended thirty, I placed his wrist back down, not wanting to touch him anymore and stood up.

"He's dead?" she asked, and I nodded, confirming what Callie believed. "What do we do?"

"Let's get out of this room," I suggested. I decided we could both use a breather to collect ourselves. Since there was nothing we could do to save the guy, there was no reason for us to be in the same room as him.

I guided Callie and Pyrus all the way out of the bakery. I could see that the fresh air helped a little, some of the color coming back to Callie's face, but she still seemed rather pale.

"How are you feeling?" I asked her.

"Better," she answered.

I didn't want to wait too long to get the police out here. I kept my eyes on Callie while I dialed 911.

"Who are you calling?" Callie asked.

"The police."

"Right, right." Callie nodded absentmindedly. I spoke to the operator, giving her all the necessary information. I kept an eye on Callie the entire time. She was the one I was most worried about. I should've gotten her a glass of water or something because she did not look good.

Suddenly, Callie turned to me, her complexion pallid.

"Lydia, I, um…" Before she could finish, her body started to fall to the ground. I had to drop my phone to catch her.

"Callie!" I wasn't able to fully stop her fall, but I helped her reach the ground a lot slower. As I gently laid her down, Pyrus pushed my phone over to me, and I picked it up. I could hear the operator calling my name. She was asking if everything was alright. I sat down with Callie's head in my lap and took my phone from Pyrus.

"Hi, sorry. My assistant just passed out. I think the stress was too much for her. Could you send someone to check her over as well?" I was able to catch her fast enough so she hadn't hit her head, but it would still probably be a good idea for her to get her head checked out.

"Of course. I've sent your information over to the local police station and EMTs, and they should be with you shortly."

"Thank you." I hung up my phone, placing it next to me on the ground. I moved Callie's hair from her face, hoping it would do something to cool her down. Pyrus curled up near us, resting her head on Callie's stomach. Her breathing was evening out which was a good sign.

"It's going to be okay," I whispered to Callie. She wasn't awake yet, but her body did seem to relax a little at my words.

It didn't take long for me to hear the approaching sirens.

Chapter Four

"What happened!" Callie startled in my arms. She sat up and looked in the direction of the approaching emergency vehicles.

"You passed out," I informed her. Callie looked at me confused, then over at the bakery.

"Is there really— Are they coming because—" Callie stammered, unable to get a full sentence out.

"Yeah, that happened."

"Jeez..." Callie muttered. Moments later an ambulance and a police car pulled up. I helped Callie up as the EMTs and police got out of their vehicles. I walked her over to the ambulance, so she could be looked over. She kept insisting she was fine, but I'd rather be safe than sorry.

While the EMTs tended to Callie, Trish Lloyd and a man I had never seen before walked over. Because we were such a small town, our police force was small. Trish and I went to school together, and I wasn't at all surprised when she joined the Park Perdsor Police Department. Her father was on the force, and she had followed in his footsteps.

The police department had incidents here and there that kept them busy. In a small town like ours, little disputes cropped up often. Usually, it didn't need to go as far as an arrest, but every once in a while, someone would get put in holding to cool down.

That being said, there hadn't been a murder in Park Perdsor for years. I knew the news would spread quickly, and by the end of the day, everyone in town would know.

Hopefully, we wouldn't get too many looky loos.

But this new person with Trish. This *unknown* person. He was intriguing.

And not just because he was cute.

Which he was.

Just a little.

But he was also new. And new was interesting.

"Lydia," Trish greeted me. "This is Isaak Wells, our new detective."

"Detective?" Had we ever had a detective? I wasn't intimately aware of the ins and outs of the Park Perdsor Police Department, but I was pretty sure that we'd never had a detective. And if we did, they never looked like this guy.

He looked like he just came off the set of *Law & Order*. Suit and all.

"Yep, the big boys in the city decided our town could use a detective, so they sent this one down."

Isaak nodded dryly at Trish's joke. "That's me. Head Detective Wells."

I glanced over at Trish. She didn't seem bothered by Isaak's curtness, so I decided I wouldn't be bothered by it.

Detective Wells took out a small notepad and looked between me and Callie. "Which one of you found the body?"

"I did," Callie offered, raising her hand.

"I walked in a few minutes later, so I can show you." I'd rather not make Callie relive that trauma. Especially if it would cause her to pass out again.

"Sure." Isaak shrugged. "Trish, why don't you talk to..." Isaak looked at Callie, waiting.

"Callie."

"Why don't you talk to Callie, and I'll go inside with..." And then he turned to me.

"Lydia."

"I'll go inside with Lydia."

"And Pyrus."

"Pyrus?"

"My dog!" Pyrus came out from her hiding spot, and I picked her up to show Isaak. They just stared at each other for a few moments before Isaak turned his gaze back to me.

"Are you ready?" His lack of enthusiasm at meeting Pyrus was duly noted and fully disappointing, but I soldiered on, giving him the benefit of the doubt. There was a dead body waiting for us inside, and maybe he was more focused on that.

"Yeah, let's go."

With Pyrus securely in my grasp, I led Isaak to the body. He circled the dead man, giving the whole scene a thorough search.

"What time did you find him?"

"Um, we got here a little before eight, so around then?"

"Did you see anyone suspicious hanging out around recently?"

"Suspicious? What do you mean?"

Isaak looked up from his notebook and at me like I just said the stupidest thing he had ever heard. I put Pyrus down, so I could cross my arms and give him some of that attitude back.

"Someone you didn't know. Someone you didn't expect to see. Anything out of the ordinary."

"No, I didn't see any of that."

"O-kay," he noted my answer. "Do you know the deceased?"

"No, I've never seen him before."

So, how the hell did he get in here? I didn't see any broken—

"So, how did he get in here?" Isaak tapped his pen on his notebook, his words interrupting my thoughts.

"That's exactly what I was thinking about." It was kind of weird that he voiced the exact thought I was having at the exact moment I was having it.

"Good thought," he responded. The ghost of a smile appeared on his face, but we weren't able to savor the moment because I heard some scratching noises. I looked down, and Pyrus wasn't at my feet.

"Uh oh!" I looked around and found the end of her leash.

"What—" Isaak followed my line of sight to my errant dog. "She'd better not be disturbing the crime scene!"

"She's nowhere near the body," I mumbled, but I was also panicking, rushing over to pick her up. She was being more finicky than usual, still going for something under the table. "I think there's something under there."

"It's probably just a treat you dropped or something."

I gave Isaak an annoyed look. "Well, I'm going to check it out."

"Wait!" Isaak held up his hands. "Let me." He took off his suit jacket, folding it and placing it on the counter before rolling up his sleeves. I quickly grabbed Pyrus, holding her close to my chest and taking a step back. I was, embarrassingly enough, stunned into silence by the man's very attractive physique. It was the second time I noticed how nice he looked, and I was starting to get on my own nerves.

Pyrus and I watched as Isaak got down on the floor and reached underneath the table. From where I was standing, I got a very good look at his rear end.

And it was one of the nicer ones I'd seen in my life.

Maybe I could get used to his slightly annoying ways.

Isaak pulled his hand back and stood up.

"I think this is what she found." It was a key. It actually looked like the key to the bakery.

"That is one of my keys... to the bakery. I must have dropped it."

"Oh, here you go. You'll probably need that." Isaak handed me the key. I looked at it confused, because I had no idea how it could have gotten under the table.

"What is it?" Isaak asked as he swiped the dirt and dust that he picked up from the floor off his clothes.

"It's just—" Before I could answer, Pyrus was yapping, jumped out of my arms, and ran away. Isaak and I followed her to a window in the back that I hadn't seen when I first came in. There was broken glass all over the floor. I quickly picked her up again, so she wouldn't step on the shards.

"This must be where he broke in," Isaak concluded. He turned to Pyrus, a big smile on his face. "What a helpful pup." He gave her a quick scratch on the head.

But I wasn't convinced. Something didn't feel right.

"Why would he break in here? Of all places?"

"What do you mean?"

"Well, it's not the most obvious spot. It's a bit of a hidden window and not the easiest to climb into. Why not break in through the front? Or use the backdoor?" If he really did break in, then I felt like it would make more sense to break the door window to try and unlock it. That way, he'd be able to walk in.

"He probably used it because it was more hidden, and maybe he cased the joint before deciding to rob it."

"Maybe..."

Isaak's answer still wasn't enough for me because why would he rob a store that wasn't even open yet. If he was casing it, he would've known that we'd been closed the entire time, so what could he have been after?

And more importantly, who had killed him?

"Look, we'll investigate and get to the bottom of this. If there are any developments, I promise to let you know."

"Thank you. I appreciate that."

"Here." Isaak pulled out his wallet and handed me a card. "You can call me if you have any questions or need to talk about what happened here."

I tentatively took his card. "You want me to call just to... talk?"

His cheeks got a little red which made me smile on the inside. "I know something like this can be traumatizing, and I wanted to offer support if you need it. Or you could talk to Trish if that makes you more comfortable."

"No, no. I'll call *you* if I wake up in a cold sweat."

"Yeah, okay." He chuckled. Isaak's phone pinged, and he checked it. "The medical examiner is here. He's going to look over the body and then we'll remove it from the premises. You'll need to hire a certified cleaning crew—"

"Cleaning crew. I have to hire a cleaning crew?"

"Well, you don't *have* to, but given that this is a bakery, I don't think you'll pass inspection without one. I've also seen people try to do it themselves, and it rarely works out."

"Okay, fine, but I have to pay for it?"

"Well, yeah." He said it so casually. Why should I have to pay for the cleaning service when I had nothing to do with said murder. Was the cost of the window going to come out of my pocket too?

"And I won't get reimbursed or anything?" Isaak shook his head. "That's idiotic!"

"Once we apprehend the murderer, and they are convicted, you can sue them for any costs—"

"So, more work for me. You'd think they would have come up with a better system by now." I knew the dead guy on my kitchen floor was having a much worse day, but I couldn't help but be a little upset with him for having to die in *my* bakery.

"I can send you some good ones in the area..."

"Yeah. Thanks." I was back to being curt because I was annoyed. Maybe my insurance would cover it, but that still meant filing a claim, and going through bureaucratic hell. No matter what route I took, I ended up losing.

"Yep. No problem." Isaak returned my curtness, but I didn't even care. I had too much to deal with to worry about him. We left the bakery and rejoined Trish and Callie outside.

"You done in there?" Trish asked.

"Yeah, I'm gonna wait in the car." Isaak didn't even wait before heading to his car.

"Whad'ya do to him?" Trish asked me.

"Nothing. I'm just annoyed because I just found out *I* have to pay for a cleaning crew."

"They never show you that part on TV," Trish joked. "We might have some extra money in the budget to help you if you need it."

"Really, that'd be a huge help." Then I frowned, realizing Isaak had been way less helpful. "Why didn't the detective mention this?"

"He's a little more by the book. Hasn't quite gotten the hang of how we do things out here, but I think he's almost there." I turned and scowled at Isaak sitting in his car. He made a face back at me before looking away.

"Well, his ignorance almost cost me."

"I'm not making any promises, Lydia. We might not be able to cover the whole thing either, but just help offset the cost. I'll get back to you once I find out, okay?" I understood. I thanked Trish for her help and said goodbye to her.

I checked in on Callie. The EMTs had given her a look over and said she was fine. The medical examiner had just pulled in, and Isaak was talking to her. I wasn't sure how much longer this whole thing was going to take, and I did not want to be waiting around for them to finish.

"Ya hungry?" I asked Callie.

"I could eat." She shrugged.

"Why don't we get out of here? Come back when it's less crowded."

Callie nodded, some of the tension leaving her body. "I like that idea. Could use a breather." Before we left, I asked Trish to text me when they were done. The diner wasn't too far of a walk, and I thought it would do all of us some good, so I had the three of us—Callie, Pyrus, and myself—walk over.

I'd deal with the mess in my bakery later.

Chapter Five

It took us about twenty-five minutes to get to the diner. It was because my *dog* kept wandering off to pee or sniff something. But I was patient with her, and the slow pace seemed to be working for Callie as well. I felt less waves of anxiety rolling off of her, and by the time we reached Sal's, she was in a much better place.

"Ready to eat?" I asked. Callie nodded.

"That walk made me even hungrier." I smiled as we went inside. Park Perdsor had a few eateries, but Sal's was the most popular. It had been here the longest, opening up only a few years after the town's founding. It had gone through numerous name and aesthetic changes, but the moniker of Sal's had lasted some decades. Taken from the last name of the family that owned it "Sal" was short for Saling, and the current owners were twins, Peter and Polly Saling. Polly led the kitchen while Peter ran things up in the front.

"Lydia!" Peter called my name as Callie, Pyrus, and I entered.

"Peter, hey!" He gave me a quick hug before leaning in to whisper.

"I heard the news. I'm so sorry." I knew what happened this morning would spread like wildfire, but I thought it would take longer than twenty-five minutes.

Until I remembered that Trish and Peter were dating.

Jeez, Trish.

"Thank you, Peter. I really appreciate it."

"Please let us treat you today." I wasn't about to say no to a free meal, so I gladly accepted his offer. Peter then turned to Callie. "And who is this?"

"Peter, Callie. Callie, Peter. Callie is my new assistant at the bakery."

"Well, it's nice to meet you. Y'all can sit wherever, and I'll be over to take your order soon." Peter headed for the kitchen, no doubt to update Polly on all the "drama". The Salings were nice, but boy, did they love gossip.

I placed Pyrus in the booth next to me before picking a menu and looking it over. I'd been to Sal's hundreds of times, but I would always look at the menu. It was a habit at that point.

I found what I wanted to order, some pancakes with sausage, and also picked something out for Pyrus. I put the menu down and looked over at Callie. She was staring out the window. I followed her line of sight and saw Lionel Turner, our local real estate developer.

"Are you okay?" Callie jumped out of her seat at the sound of my voice. "Sorry, I didn't mean to scare you."

"No, I'm fine. I was just thinking about…"

I nodded, knowing exactly what Callie was talking about. She didn't need to say it out loud if she didn't want to.

"Do you want to talk about it?"

"No." She shook her head. "I just need some time to think is all." Callie sighed. I fully understood. Peter soon came over and took our orders. While we waited for our meals, Lionel entered the diner.

Lionel and I were on… good terms. He was the one who sold me the bakery. He owned some property in Park Perdsor, but he was looking to expand and wanted to offload some of the land he owned so he could focus on other ventures. I had to get a hefty loan from the bank to purchase the property from Lionel, but I wanted to own instead of rent. Things felt more secure that way. Negotiations had gotten a little hairy between the two of us at times, but the ink had dried, so it was all behind us.

Though it wasn't easy to just push away some of those hard feelings. Clearly, Lionel was a businessman before anything else, and I just learned to respect that. I also kept my distance.

But that distance was getting smaller because he was approaching our table.

"Lydia, it's nice to see you!"

"It's nice to see you too, Lionel." I smiled. "Have you heard what's happened?"

Lionel's brow furrowed as he shook his head. I told him about what happened this morning, just giving the rundown of the main points because I didn't want to get too far into it.

"Callie and I have no idea who the guy is or why he was there. I'm just hoping the police are able to resolve this whole thing soon." Lionel glanced at Callie, and that was when I realized I hadn't introduced them. "Oh, and this is Callie. She's my new assistant. Callie, this is Lionel. He's the one who sold me the bakery."

Callie offered Lionel a sheepish hello, barely looking at him. I internally chastised myself for not being more in tune with her. She had just said she didn't want to talk about what went on this morning, and there I was, going on and on.

Thankfully, Peter soon came over with our food, and I was able to end my conversation with Lionel. Once our food was on the table, and the three of us were alone again, I apologized to Callie.

"I am so sorry. We are here to decompress and not think about all that bad stuff."

"It's fine. Don't worry about it."

"Thank you for that, but I want to respect your requests. We're gonna be working together. Hopefully for a long time. I never want you to feel like I am steamrolling over your feelings or ignoring what you say to me."

"Yeah, no..." Callie paused. She seemed deep in thought. "Thank you. I really appreciate it." We finally dug into our food, and I asked Callie questions about her life. She was in the middle of telling me about her college years when we were interrupted by a phone call.

I took my phone out and saw a number I did not recognize.

"Do you mind...?" Callie gestured that she didn't care, so I answered. "Hello?"

"Lydia? This is Detective Wells." So formal. Strange.

"Hello, Detective Wells. To what do I owe this pleasure?" There was a hint of sarcasm in my voice. It had just been over an hour since he'd annoyed me, and I wasn't quite over it yet.

"I was calling because we were able to identify the man found in your bakery. His name was Thomas Yondle. We got the ID from his fingerprints which were in the system due to his pretty extensive rap sheet." *Thomas Yondle?* I'd never heard that name before.

"What was he arrested for?"

"A few things. Drug possession, distribution, assault. He was actually recently released from prison a little over a month ago." That was depressing to hear. Only out of jail a month, and he'd already fallen victim to his own bad habits. I understood that he might have broken into my bakery to rob me, but I felt bad that he died.

"Okay, so he was in my bakery to steal something?"

"That's the working hypothesis. He probably was looking for money or maybe he thought he could sell some of the equipment."

"I guess, but it doesn't make sense. We weren't open yet, so there wouldn't have been any money yet. There's so many other places he could've gone that were right there." My bakery wasn't quite on Main Street, but it wasn't far from the other businesses. Ones that would have just made more sense. "And do you have any idea who he was with?"

"We're looking into his known associates. He probably got in with his old crew after he got out and things went south. And drug addicts aren't known for being the most logical." I wondered if Isaak could hear all the contradictions he was throwing my way. First, he said that Thomas must have cased my bakery, looking for just the right time to strike, but on this call, he was going on about how Thomas and his partner must not have thought this crime through.

The dots weren't connecting!

"Isaak, I don't know—"

"Also, I found the list of cleaning companies. I'll send it to you shortly. The ME's office already took the body, and hopefully we'll be able to sign off on the scene by the end of the day, so you can get it all cleaned up. I'll call you if there are any further developments." Isaak hung up on me, and I was left feeling like the whole case was going nowhere.

"So, what did the detective have to say?"

"Nothing particularly helpful. Turns out the man who broke in has been to jail quite a few times. Detective *Wells* thinks that he was looking for money to buy drugs, or he re-joined his old crew, and yeah…" I stabbed my fork into my pancakes, taking a frustrated bite.

"And you don't think that's what's going on?"

"Not really. Too many things aren't adding up, but I'm not the detective, so…" I shrugged.

Callie and I finished our meals. I knew I had a lot of things to sort out with getting the bakery cleaned up and our grand opening approaching, but I was sooooo tired.

"What are you going to do next?"

"I think I'm going to go home. I can't take care of stuff at the bakery until tomorrow at the earliest. Today, I actually need to get some baking done. I'm already behind on some of my online orders." The online orders were keeping me afloat. Without them, my little bakery would have been dead in the water much earlier.

"If you want some help, I've seemed to have found myself free for the day," Callie offered.

"Callie Pierson! Was that a joke?" I laughed. It would appear Callie had a wicked sense of humor. She shrugged. "I might just take you up on that offer. Just know, we are about to do a lot of baking. Are you up to being elbow deep in batter?"

"Throw me in, coach!"

I laughed again. I waved goodbye to Peter as we left the diner. Callie followed me back to my house, so that we could get to baking.

Chapter Six

We got back to my place, and I showed Callie around my modest home. Once we were done with the grand tour which consisted of my living room, kitchen, bedroom, spare room, and semi-finished basement, I put Pyrus in the living room and gave Callie a rundown of everything we needed to get done.

"I thought you were exaggerating about how much baking we'd be doing." Callie looked at all the ingredients I'd pulled out. When I said elbow deep, I meant it.

"It isn't too late to back out."

Callie shook her head. "No, I'm here to help and to learn. Let's do this."

I already had a game plan for the order to do things. I divided up the tasks between Callie and myself, making sure not to leave her with anything too overwhelming.

With some music playing in the background, Callie and I got to work. I had to show her a few things here and there, but she was a quick study and did good work. Baking with Callie was a bright spot in a pretty dreary day, knowing that I picked correctly for my assistant.

"So, what got you into baking?"

"Um, well..." Callie paused for a few seconds. "It's kind of sad, but my mom didn't really have a lot of time to *do* stuff for me, so I kinda learned to cook myself, and that eventually led to learning how to bake." Callie looked down at the dough she was kneading while she told me this.

Callie seemed to have some sadness surrounding her. Many people did, to a degree, but I had sensed that she held some deep wounds. Given that our relationship barely spanned forty-eight hours, I didn't feel like it was my place to pry, but I was curious.

"How are things with you and your mom now?"

"They're... complicated. We actually got into an argument before I moved down here. She didn't want me to."

"Why?"

"Her memories of this place aren't as good as mine," she mumbled. I could tell we were getting into sensitive territory, so I pulled back on my questions.

"Well, I'm glad you're here. You have no idea how much of a godsend you have been for me." Without Callie, dealing with everything that had happened would have been so much harder. I thought about what it would have been like, baking all alone. I enjoyed baking, but it was also my job which meant sometimes it got annoying.

If I was doing all of these orders alone, I would have been in such a mood. Instead, I was having a pretty good time.

"I'm really happy to be working with you. I've never had such a nice boss." She smiled.

"How many bosses have you had?"

"A handful. What about you? Have you always done this?"

I shook my head. "Nope. I had all kinds of jobs throughout the years. It was only recently that I started baking full-time."

"It's so cool that you can support yourself doing this."

"Well," I started. It was true that my bills were paid, but it was always such a to-do when it came to budgeting and moving money around. It was a living. A stressful living, but one I was glad to have. "Let's just say I get by."

Callie and I continued in the kitchen until everything was made and then packed away. She helped me label all the boxes. We collapsed onto the chairs I had in my kitchen, covered in flour and exhausted.

"We did it." I smiled.

"Do you want me to drop anything off?" Callie asked.

"Oh my goodness, Callie. We just spent hours toiling away in the kitchen, and you're ready to work some more?" My body felt ready to not move for at least a week.

"I just want to help if I can."

"I know, I know. And I really appreciate it, but I like to think one of the best parts about working super hard is getting to relax afterwards. Which is why I think," I got up from my seat and went to the fridge, pulling out a bottle of wine I had chilling inside, "we should drink this." I held the bottle up to show Callie.

"That does sound nice..."

"Then let's pop it open!" I grabbed two wine glasses and the wine opener, and motioned for Callie to follow me into the living room so we'd be able to really get comfy on the couch.

I was about to sit my bottom down when Callie stopped me.

"Wait! What about the..." She motioned to flour on our clothes.

Right...

"You know what, we're at my house. I've got extra clothes upstairs!" I put the wine down, took Callie's hand, and led her upstairs. Minutes later, we were back downstairs in clean clothes, and I was pouring a glass of wine for both of us.

I took a satisfying sip of my wine and got cozy.

"So, what's the plan for tomorrow?"

"I'm going to get these deliveries to the post office. Some are pretty close, but I don't know if I'll be up for driving all over the area." I still had to get the cleaners situated and figure out if the grand opening could even happen as scheduled.

I could already tell it was going to be a tough week.

"Do you want me to come into the bakery?"

I shook my head. "No, don't worry about it. Take the day off, and we can talk about everything in two days. Or if you need more time off, please let me know. I understand if this whole thing has really shaken you up." I should have probably taken some time off myself, but keeping busy was always how I dealt with things.

"I'll be ready to go in two days. I could work tomorrow, but I will take it off."

I was glad Callie was taking my offer to have the day off. We'd already worked super hard today, and she'd earned it.

"If you're looking for something to do outside of visiting the lighthouse, there is a beautiful cove at the end of the beach. They recently put up markers to help direct people because tourists started going in and getting lost." While the cove wasn't super hard to get to, it wasn't an immediately obvious destination, so only the locals really went, and we all just knew how to navigate it. Knowledge passed down through the generations. We still weren't sure who'd spilled the beans, but over the past few years, more and more out-of-towners had been making their way to the cove.

After one of them got lost, the city council quickly voted to put up signs. They didn't want to risk it. If I didn't think Callie could navigate it by herself, I'd go with her for her first time, but I felt like the cove was another nice place to think, when it wasn't too crowded.

"Okay, I'll check it out!" We spoke for a little bit longer before I sent Callie home for the night. I gave her some brownies and promised to check in with her tomorrow night. There was still some work I could have tackled, but I decided that I had done enough for the day.

"Pyrus!" I called out. She entered the living room moments later. I gave her dinner before heading upstairs and getting myself ready for bed. As I emptied my pocket, I pulled out the key that Pyrus had found earlier.

"I'd forgotten about you..."

I had no idea where it came from. There were three sets of keys for the bakery. I had one on my key ring, a set I planned on giving to Callie, and a spare set. I checked my drawer and found the spare set, but I never did give Callie the keys. I was sure those ones were still in my car since I'd never taken them out because of all of the commotion.

I could have settled with that conclusion, but I needed to double-check. I quickly ran outside to my car and checked my center console.

"They're still here." I was stumped. There shouldn't be a fourth set of keys. Lionel had given me all the keys he had when he sold me the property, and given all the renovations I had done on the bakery, I would have found these in those early days.

Right?

Maybe not...

It could have gotten lost before. A forgotten key. It probably meant nothing.

But did anything ever really mean nothing? I decided to put the key away for the time being. If it became relevant later, then I'd still have it. I went back inside and headed to bed.

Chapter Seven

The next day, I started my day with getting the completed orders to the post office. I left Pyrus in the car while I got everything sent out.

"A lot of packages today," Gage commented. Gage was one of our local mailmen and ran Park Perdsor's USPS location. He was a few years older than me, so we never went to school together. We got to know each other when we got older. He helped me navigate the right ways to send food through the mail. I wanted to make sure everything was up to standard—didn't want anybody getting sick or to find myself in an FDA nightmare.

I'd always bring him a treat as a perpetual thank you for all the help he gave me.

"Yeah, I got a little behind on orders, but I hired a new assistant and we buckled down last night and baked our little hearts out which means I have this for you." I pulled out the Danish I made for Gage. He accepted it with glee.

"Is it—"

"Raspberry, your favorite."

"Uh, you are absolutely amazing."

I smiled at the compliment before handing everything I wanted to send out to Gage. We double checked all of the addresses, and then he got everything into the system.

"I emailed you all the tracking numbers, and they'll also be on your receipt. You know the drill."

"That I do." Trips to the post office weren't always my favorite thing to do. I loved seeing Gage and catching up with him, but we could always catch up at Sal's where there was beer and food. Maybe it was my fault that so many of our conversations happened while he was at work. I barely had time for myself, so that meant having even less time for my friends. Gage was always inviting me out, and I was always declining.

But once things settled with the bakery, we would totally hang out.

But there were definitely worse things to be stuck doing.

Gage went quiet for a moment, and I had a feeling I knew where he was going. It was the talk of the town, and what everyone was focused on.

"So, I heard about what happened yesterday."

"And what happened yesterday?" I wasn't about to let Gage get his gossip that easy. He had to work for it. Just a little.

"I heard a murder, maybe? In your bakery."

"That about sums it up." And it was really all I knew so far. There hadn't been any updates yet, but it also hadn't been that long. I was sure they'd be calling soon.

"It's just so crazy."

"Yeah, it was quite the shock. I just hope that Trish is able to close the case quickly." That was something else I would need to take care of. Could I open my bakery before the case was closed? Isaak did say they were handing the "scene" back to me, but what exactly did that mean? And in what state would I be getting my bakery back?

"Just Trish?"

"Huh?" I had no idea what Gage meant by that comment.

"I said just Trish? I thought there was another person at the station. Newly hired, very handsome. Came all the way from the city."

Oh, he was talking about Isaak.

"You mean Detective Wells."

"So you have met him." Gage chuckled. "Sounds like somebody has a crush."

I could feel my face making the ugliest expression because how did he come to *that* conclusion?

"I do not have a crush. I don't even like him!"

Gage laughed. "That's how I know you have a crush. Every time you like someone, you always get into these weird arguments with them, and then you get all grumpy whenever they're mentioned. It's a vicious cycle really.."

I was about to make a retort, but then I stopped myself and thought about what he said. Did I really argue with people like that?

I pouted like a child because I didn't like an observation like that being made about me. *I* was meant to be the observant one.

"Whatever," I grumbled. "Enjoy your Danish."

"I will!" I left the post office and got into my car, heading back home.

"Gage was just pulling my leg, right?" I glanced at Pyrus. She just looked back at me. It made me feel put on the spot. I didn't have a crush on *Detective Wells*. Gage was just teasing me because that's the kind of guy Gage was. I'd been single for quite some time, and my friends just wanted me to find someone nice.

I wasn't against the idea of having a partner, but it had to be the right person. I wasn't of the mind that Detective Wells was the right person. How well did Gage know him anyway? He probably got it all second-hand from Trish, and she was sometimes known to embellish at times.

"That's what that was. A joke. A great big joke." I pushed the conversation out of my mind, not wanting to dwell on it any longer. It was only a big deal if I made it a big deal.

We finally got home, and as I pulled into my driveway, I heard something go thud in the backseat.

"What was that?" Pyrus hopped into the back of the car and went under the chair. I could hear her pawing at something. I got out of my seat and went to the back. "Let me get it."

Pyrus moved out of the way, so I could reach under the seat. I felt around and pulled out the mystery object.

"Oh, crap…" It was one of my deliveries. I checked the address on the box, and it wasn't *that* far away. Yes, it was in Connecticut, so I'd be crossing state lines, but the drive wasn't a bad one. Without traffic, it would take me about two hours to get there. Maybe two and half if I had to make any stops. And that way I wouldn't have to see Gage again and deal with his teasing.

Also, a drive could help me clear my head a little. Gage's comment had got to me a lot more than I would have liked to admit.

"Wanna go for a drive, Pyrus?"

"Woof!" she answered, waving her tail.

It looked like we were both in agreement. I went inside to grab her some treats and then took Pyrus on a quick walk, so she could pee before we left. Satisfied that Pyrus would last for the two-hour ride, we hopped in the car and got back on the road.

"In a quarter of a mile, turn right onto Hancock Street."

We were about ten minutes away from the delivery. My prediction about the drive had been right.

When we hit the highway, I rolled down the windows and turned up the showtunes. The tension I'd been feeling just under two hours ago was pretty much gone. A few gallons of gas wasn't a bad price to pay, and the drive back would probably be similar, so I had that to look forward to.

I followed the GPS until we reached our destination.

"890 Pine Street." The package was addressed to a Georgina Hayes. "Let's take this woman her treats!" I leashed up Pyrus, and we headed to the porch. I considered ringing the doorbell to see if there was anyone at home to hand the package to, but I decided against it. It would be easier to just leave it by the front door.

While I was looking for the right spot, I heard a voice that stopped me in my tracks.

"Lydia?"

I turned around and saw Detective Wells walking towards me. Of all the people in the world...

"Detective Wells?"

What in the world was he doing there? We were two hours outside of Park Perdsor. There was no way we just both ended up here. The circumstances simply could not be that good.

"What are you doing here?"

"What are *you* doing here?" My question sounded like an accusation, but I couldn't comprehend how we both ended up at this random address at the same time. My mind was literally reeling. It was messing with me a little bit.

"Lydia." Isaak's voice dropped an octave like it was a warning, and in that moment, I remembered he was a cop and I was just a person.

I held up the package in my hand. "I'm here to deliver this."

Isaak tried to take it, and I instinctually pulled it back.

"What is it?" he asked.

"Just some cookies. I run a baking business, remember?"

"I remember," he answered. The way he said it made me shift uncomfortably. It was like he was admitting to knowing intimate details about me, but it was nowhere close to that. I had to look away for a second. I took a deep breath and turned my gaze back on Isaak.

"What are you doing here?" I asked. I needed to know how we both found ourselves on this porch. Isaak opened his mouth to talk, but before I could hear his answer, the door opened behind me.

"Hello?"

I turned around and saw who I assumed was Georgina Hayes.

Isaak and I both said hi at the same time. We glanced at one another, and then I quickly made the choice to let Isaak do the talking, given he was the cop.

"Hi, my name is Detective Wells. You are Georgina Hayes?"

"Is this about Tommy?"

"Can we come in?"

We? We! I hid my surprise at the fact that Isaak wanted me to go inside with him because I didn't want to alarm Georgina, but I didn't know why Isaak would want me to go with him.

Unless it was to keep an eye on me.

How annoying...

"Yeah, sure." Georgina opened her door more and moved aside to let us in.

"Is it okay if I bring my dog?" I asked. That was when both Isaak and Georgina saw that Pyrus was there for the first time.

"Yeah, it's not a problem." I picked up Pyrus and entered the house with Isaak. As Georgina led us through her house, I remembered that she asked

Isaak if his visit was about Tommy. I started putting two and two together and realized that we were most likely in the home of Thomas Yondle. The man that was found dead in my bakery yesterday.

Oh boy...

Chapter Eight

Isaak and I sat down next to one another on the couch while Georgina sat across from us.

"Do you want anything? Water, tea, coffee? We also have lemonade."

"No, I'm fine, thank you," Isaak answered.

"I'm fine as well." I was too uncomfortable to drink anything. If Isaak was about to do what I thought he was about to do… this woman's whole world was about to be shattered.

Isaak reached into his pocket to pull out his notebook, and that was when I realized we were sitting *quite* close to one another. I scooted over a little bit to give us some space. Isaak furrowed his brow in confusion, but he didn't say anything, instead turning to Georgina.

"I'm here because I have some unfortunate news."

I noticed that Georgina's hands were shaking. She grabbed them, planting them in her lap.

"Where did you find him?" she asked, her voice grave.

"I'm sorry?"

"I'm assuming he's overdosed. You're here to tell me that he died somewhere with a needle in his arm."

Her candor caught me off-guard. Georgina's eyes turned to me, and she must have seen my surprise. She gave me a tired smile.

"I've been with Tommy ever since we were kids. I always saw the best in him, but almost two decades with an addict... Well, this isn't a visit I'm surprised is happening." I understood where she was coming from, but knowing that it wasn't quite as she pictured... my heart sank waiting for Isaak to deliver the news.

"We did find him, but it wasn't an overdose," Isaak started. "We're actually not totally sure what happened, but we are investigating."

Georgina furrowed her brow in confusion. "What are you talking about?"

"Yesterday, we found Tommy's body in a storefront in Park Perdsor. We believe he was murdered."

Georgina leaned back in her seat, hugging her body. I watched as a flurry of emotions flashed across her face as she processed what Isaak had just told her.

"He was murdered? By who?"

"We don't know yet. I was hoping you might know the people he's been around recently."

"I-I don't know!" Tears started forming at the edges of Georgina's eyes. I wished there was something I could do or say to make her feel better, but the grief she was feeling was too easy to be consumed by.

"We have been looking into his known associates, but we haven't found much there."

"You talked to Jimmy?"

"Jimmy?"

"Jimmy Tate. He and Tommy are buddies from an old job. They used to get high together, but Jimmy got clean a few years back, and they fell out, but Tommy's been pretty committed to getting clean, so they've been talking again. He lives out of state, but he might know something..." Georgina looked down into her lap, picking at her nails. "Ever since Tommy got out, things had actually been really good. He was going to NA meetings, he'd cut off his old crew. He even had a new job. I didn't want to get my hopes up because he's disappointed me so many times, but this time felt different. I don't know." She shrugged.

Georgina suddenly stood up, running her hands through her hair.

"Could you excuse me for a moment?" She didn't wait for an answer and left the room. I awkwardly looked over at Isaak who had settled into the couch as he rubbed his eyes.

"Are you okay?" I asked him.

"Yeah, I'm fine. It just never gets easier."

"What?"

"Telling people their loved ones aren't coming home." I nodded. I'd only ever been on the receiving end back when my mom died. I couldn't imagine having to do this kind of thing as a job.

"I think you're doing a pretty good job," I offered.

"Thanks." Isaak and I looked at one another, sharing what felt like an intimate moment, but it was cut short when Georgina walked back into the room.

"Sorry, I just…"

"Perfectly understandable," I said. There was no reason for her to have to explain herself. Especially to us.

"Um, could I get Jimmy's contact info?" Isaak asked.

"Of course." Georgina rattled off a phone number that Isaak scribbled down. She continued to fidget in her chair but then suddenly stopped. She took a deep breath and turned to Isaak.

"You said he was found in Park Perdsor?" Isaak nodded. "Where is that?"

"It's in Rhode Island about two or two and a half hours away," I commented.

"What was he doing there?" Georgina mumbled.

"I was hoping you might know. There was nothing in his file to connect him to the place. I thought you might have some answers."

Georgina shrugged. She held her hand over her mouth as she thought. "He was in and out a lot the past few months. He wouldn't tell me much, just that he was going to work, and I was just happy that he was doing something. After Tommy got out of jail, he would stay inside all day. I could tell he was depressed, which for an addict is not a good state. I was just trying to maintain the good times…"

Georgina's voice caught in her throat, and she took a moment before continuing.

"I should have asked more questions, but he hated it when I micromanaged him." Georgina chuckled sadly to herself. "Do you have any idea who did this?"

Isaak shook his head. "We don't even really know why he was in town. I'm hoping we'll be able to put the pieces together soon."

"I hope you do. I want to know who hurt him. I want them to pay."

A silence fell over the room. After a few beats of awkwardness, Isaak cleared his throat.

"I don't want to take up anymore of your time. If you have any more questions, you can reach me here." Isaak took out a card that was the same as he had given me the other day and passed it on to Georgina. "Or if you remember something that you feel is relevant."

"Yeah, got it." She placed the card on the table. We all stood up at the same time. Isaak and I were about to leave when Georgina stopped us. "Oh, don't forget your…" That was when she looked down at the box and saw her name.

"Oh! That's actually for you. I was delivering it."

"You were… delivering?" She looked between me and Isaak. "You're not with him?"

"Um, no. I know him. I was just... it was..." I wasn't sure what to say. Was it appropriate to tell Georgina that Tommy was found in *my* bakery. She might think I was just some nosy weirdo tagging along. As I scrambled to come up with an explanation, Isaak did it for me.

"Lydia is helping me with the investigation. She is also from Park Perdsor, and she's..."

But it would seem Isaak wasn't any better at thinking of an excuse. Not wanting to make things even more awkward, I just announced what was in the box. "They're cookies. It's an order of cookies. I'm a baker."

"Cookies, but I didn't order..." As Georgina's trailed off, realization crossed her face. She tore open the box and her eyes went wide when she saw what was inside. "You make these?"

"Uh, yeah. It's my signature recipe."

Georgina held up the box and looked between Isaak and me. "What is going on? Who are you?"

I decided that telling the truth was better than trying to get out of this. Georgina deserved the truth.

"So, Tommy was actually found in my bakery, but when I came here, I didn't know that he lived here. I just had a delivery to make, and then Isaak showed up, and it's all confusing, and I'm sorry." I spoked quickly, wanting to get it all out. My heart was beating so fiercely in my chest, I wondered if it was about to fall onto the floor.

"You found him?"

"Yeah."

"Do you know..." Georgina got choked up again, her words failing her.

"I have no idea what he was doing there. I didn't even know who he was when I saw him. I'm sorry if I've made things worse."

Georgina shook her head, wiping the tears that had escaped. "No, it's not that. I think I'm just... I don't know how to feel." She looked off into the distance, towards her backyard. "Tommy's been bringing me a box of these every week or so. He'd never tell me where he got them, just that he got them special. Just for me. He was back to doing little things like that to make me happy. It's another reason why I felt like we were doing good. It was like I was getting the old Tommy back."

"We are going to find who did this. I promise," I said.

At first, Georgina seemed confused by my statement, but she looked at my face for a few seconds, and that confusion morphed in belief. "Okay, thank you." I could tell she was being sincere. "And thank you for bringing these." She motioned to the cookies still in her hand. "It's a nice way to remember Tommy."

We said goodbye, and I made a mental note to myself to send Georgina another box of cookies with a coupon for a free lifetime supply. It was the least I could do.

Isaak followed me to my car, and as I got Pyrus situated, he spoke to me.

"Do you remember making a delivery to a Thomas Yondle or to this address?" I shook my head.

"No. Usually, I remember the names of people who order from me a lot, but his name didn't sound familiar. Neither did Georgina's." I was pretty certain I'd never seen Thomas before. "I could double-check though. I keep records as far as five years back." I could have easily missed it. Especially because I had been so busy lately with getting ready for the grand opening of the bakery.

"That's perfect. How fast could you get the info?"

"I could drive to the bakery now and send it over after I take a look?" I also wanted to head back just to see it. I hadn't been back since the police had handed the scene back to me. I was curious how much of a mess they had left.

"Amazing. I'll follow you." Isaak jogged over to his car before I could protest. While I'd rather not be in close quarters with him, it wasn't that big of a deal because I wasn't going goo goo ga ga over him. I'd make sure to quickly check the system and send Isaak on his way. My hesitation was clearly because he was exasperating. He did things like invite himself over instead of asking.

I slipped into the driver's seat and looked over at Pyrus who had curled up to relax.

"I'm totally fine," I told her. She gave me some side-eye, but I ignored the lack of belief in me. I revved up my car and pulled away from the curb.

It's not a big deal.

Chapter Nine

On the drive to the bakery, I called one of the cleaning services that Isaak recommended and was able to set up an appointment in two days. When I heard the estimate, it made my day much worse.

"Why can't anything ever work out for me, Pyrus?"

Trish still hadn't gotten back to me about whether or not there were any extra funds they'd be able to throw my way to help mitigate these rising costs. Because it wasn't just the clean-up that needed to get done. There was also a much-needed window repair given that Tommy or whoever murdered him decided to bust out one of my windows.

"I literally did nothing wrong and here I am, paying for the sins of other people. It freaking sucks!" It was another thing I decided to blame Isaak for. It would help maintain the beautiful distance that was already between us.

"We don't like that man, Pyrus. He's brought chaos into our lives!" That wasn't necessarily true. Things had been going haywire long before Isaak showed up, but sometimes it was better to live inside a delusion.

I sighed with relief when we finally pulled up to the bakery. Once parked, I unlocked the door and led Isaak to my office in the back. There was already a little area for Pyrus to hang in, so that was where she went while I booted up my computer.

"How many orders do you typically get?" Isaak asked. I was already sitting in my chair, and he was standing behind me. He was a head taller than me, but sitting down made his tallness that much more apparent. I had to actively ignore the beating of my heart as he towered over me.

"Um, it all depends on my capacity to actually bake stuff. When we 'sell out', it's not like there is a limited stock. It just means I don't want to bake that much." It was a big reason why I wanted to bring more people on. So, I could start getting more orders out. "I would say I send out a couple hundred orders in a good month." Upgrading my home oven so I could cook even bigger batches really changed the game for me, and I was sure things would get even better once I started using the kitchen at the bakery even more.

"Those numbers sound good."

"I'm able to support myself, so yeah. They are pretty good numbers."

My computer was finally on, so I logged in and pulled up the software I used to categorize my orders.

"I guess I should set the filter to only show the pear and chocolate chip cookies and organize them by name." That way I could see the repeats. "Okay, let's have a look."

Isaak looked over my shoulder as I began scrolling. I used my willpower to keep from looking over at him and seeing how close his face was to my face.

Get it together, Lydia!

"Do you see anything?"

"Not yet..." I didn't have to scroll far to find something of note. "Wait. Check this out." I pointed to the orders in question. For the past couple months, an order had been put in about once a week by a T. Yates. "That could be him. He used the same initials."

"Yeah, but why would he use a fake name? What was he trying to hide?"

I shrugged because I had no idea. All I did was sell cookies. It was perplexing. It definitely gave the impression that there was something to hide.

"What's the address for the delivery?"

"Um..." I went to the right column and read out the address to Isaak.

"Were these ones that you hand delivered?"

"No, it would seem they requested it be done through USPS." There was an option on my site for certain addresses within a certain radius to have me deliver the package myself, and they wouldn't have to pay any shipping and handling. Even though this T. Yates was on the outskirts of town, they'd decided to have everything done through the mail.

"Okay, I will definitely be checking this place out."

"Would you want company?" My curiosity won out over my desire to keep space between Isaak and myself. I wanted to know if this was in fact Tommy, and what he had to hide. Everything about it was just so mysterious.

"I can take care of this one myself. What happened back at Georgina's, that isn't what I normally do. You just caught me off-guard is all."

"So, if I catch you off-guard again, you'll let me investigate with you?" That got me a tiny smirk, but Isaak stood his ground.

"No, Lydia. I am going after a murderer. Things could get dicey, and I don't want you getting in harm's way."

"You mean getting in the way," I grumbled.

"That too." I crossed my arms over my chest, disappointed. Things were just starting to get interesting, and Isaak was shutting me out. I knew I could be helpful, if he'd just let me.

"Do you still think it was a robbery gone wrong? That he was looking for money for a fix?"

"It's the best theory." Isaak shrugged.

"I don't know. Georgina said that Tommy had been doing really well lately, and it doesn't explain why he was so far away from home." The more I thought about it, the less I liked the drug angle.

"Yes, but—"

"And what about a tox screen? I mean, were there any drugs actually found in his system?" Isaak looked at me like all the goodwill I had managed to muster was vanishing.

"We're still waiting on those results, and I'm sure when I investigate more, it'll begin making more sense. It'll just take a little work. Answers don't come out of nowhere." I narrowed my eyes at him, not liking his condescending tone.

"I know it takes work. I just don't want you working in the wrong direction."

"I will take your *ideas* into consideration, okay?"

"Fine."

"Fine." And we left it at that. Isaak finally left, and once I saw that his car was gone, I took out my phone and called Callie.

"What are you doing tonight?"

Chapter Ten

I picked Callie up from her house, and we drove over to T. Yates's address. I decided to leave Pyrus at home for the little excursion. It was late anyway, and after today's trip, she could use her beauty sleep.

When I asked Callie if she wanted to go check out a random house at midnight to see if Thomas Yondle had in fact been there, she jumped at the opportunity. It made me feel like we were kindred spirits. I wasn't sure if it was boredom or an investigative spirit that drove her, but either way, it was nice to have her along for the ride.

"What if someone's there?"

"Then we can come back during the day and knock on the door at a more reasonable hour."

"What if they're the murderer?"

"I don't know. I guess we can cross that bridge when we get there." It was something to ponder though. While I wasn't against a little thrill here and there, encountering murderers wasn't something I had on my lists of priorities.

"Everything will be fine," I reassured Callie. "I'll make sure of it."

It wasn't a long drive to the property. The houses were a little more spread out than in the part of town where I lived. I wouldn't call this area rural, but it wasn't as occupied as mine.

I parked across the street from the house, turning off my car and headlights. Callie and I stared at the dark porch.

"Do you think anyone is in there?"

"It looks pretty quiet." I couldn't really tell though, because maybe they were just asleep. "Let's go check it out." I exited the car and Callie promptly followed me. We hurried over to the porch, and I peeked into the window.

"What do you see?" Callie whispered.

"It looks empty. I don't think anyone lives here." I went over to the door and tried it, but it was locked. "Crap!"

"Let me try." I moved aside so Callie could get to the door. She pulled a small kit from her pocket and took out various... tools.

"What are those for?"

"I thought we might need to pick a lock, so I brought some stuff." I watched Callie with a renewed interest. I hadn't expected her to pull out that skill set.

Callie knelt down and started fiddling with the lock. I waited until I heard that tell-tale click. She'd done it!

"You freaking rock, Callie!" I had no idea what I would have done without her. We really were the dream team.

We tentatively entered the house. There also wasn't a car in the driveway, so I was pretty sure that no one was here. I wasn't even sure if anybody lived here, and that was only further supported as Callie and I walked around. There was barely anything in the house.

"This is weird," Callie commented, and I agreed. What could Tommy have been doing here?

"Maybe the house is under construction? Or they're renovating it?" *But then wouldn't there be tools or something?* "I'm going to look around some more." I headed into the kitchen area, hoping to find a crumb of a clue, but it was like someone had already wiped the place clean.

Maybe whoever killed Tommy was worried we'd find this place... that is if Tommy even was here.

There was still no evidence that T. Yates was indeed Tommy.

"Lydia! I think I found something!" I went back to the living room, and Callie handed me a wallet. "Look inside."

I opened it and saw Tommy's driver's license among other things.

"Where did you find this?"

"I checked behind the heater. It must have fallen or something." She shrugged. This was a big development. We had proof that Tommy had indeed been here. His link to Park Perdsor. We still didn't know why or what exactly he was doing, but it was a first stop.

"This is brilliant. You're brilliant!" I gave Callie a big hug. "We should probably head back—" Before I could get us out of there, headlights briefly illuminated the house. I glanced outside and saw a car in the driveway. "Crap! Someone's here!"

"What do we do?"

"We have to hide!"

I grabbed Callie's hand and pulled her into the nearest closet. Maybe Isaak was right about not getting mixed up in this business.

Chapter Eleven

"Are you sure this is a good idea?"

"I can't think of a better one," I admitted. There was no way out without being seen. We'd just have to wait until whoever it was left. Hopefully, they wouldn't find us while we hid.

I held onto Callie's hand as we heard the door open. Callie covered her mouth with her other hand, doing her best to suppress any sounds she was making. I'd never been in a situation more tense than this one. A murderer could have been on the other side of the door, and there was nothing we could do but wait.

If I wasn't so worried about making a sound, I'd have probably started crying. I'd be apologizing to Callie for dragging her into what might be our demise. I'd probably even do a little confession just to cover all my bases.

I listened carefully as the footsteps travelled around the room. At one point, whoever it was stopped walking, but I knew they hadn't left because we hadn't heard the door open.

What are they doing?

There was no other noise for a while. There was no way they'd just left. I was too scared to open the door and check because what if they were sitting on the floor or something? It didn't sound like they went upstairs either.

I was about to whisper *something* to Callie because we could not wait in a closet forever, when the door suddenly flew open. Callie and I screamed at the same time. I threw the wallet at whoever was in front of us and yelled for Callie to run. I was on the verge of tackling whoever was at the door, giving Callie a chance to run away, but then I saw who it was.

"Isaak?"

"Lydia! Callie! What are you doing here?" I was so relieved that it was Isaak standing in front of us and not some deranged killer that I threw my arms around him and gave him a huge hug.

"Oh, thank god!" As my adrenaline wore off, I remembered who I was embracing and quickly jumped off him. "Sorry, just relieved you're not a psycho."

"Me too." Callie smiled. Isaak looked between the two of us, the shock from my hug wearing off and turning into annoyance.

"I specifically told you not to come here."

"Yes, but I never agreed to it." Which was the truth. "I considered your advice, but I was worried you weren't going to take mine, so I wanted to check on things myself, and if we found anything, I was going to give it to you."

"That's not—"

"And we did find something!" I looked around, trying to find out where the wallet landed. "It's the thing I threw at your face... Sorry."

Callie started helping me look for it.

"What are you looking for?"

"Callie found Tommy's wallet. It proves that he was here."

"You threw his wallet at my face?" Isaak sighed. I stood upright and looked at him, offering another apology.

"I thought you were the murderer, and I'm sorry, but I also have an assistant to protect and a dog to get home to. You have to understand that."

Isaak pressed his lips into a tight line, and I noticed he was trying to keep himself from laughing, which I decided to take as a good sign.

"Found it!" We both turned to Callie who was holding up the sought-after wallet. Isaak snatched it from her hand and looked at the two of us very severely.

"This is where your investigation ends. I thank you for what you have offered so far, but please leave the police work to the police." I pouted and crossed my arms over my chest. "I need to hear you say it."

I narrowed my eyes at Isaak. He was picking up on my tricks.

"Fine. I'll leave the police work to the police," I repeated his words back to him.

"Thank you. Now go home."

Callie and I promptly left the house. On the drive back, I apologized profusely for dragging her into this mess, but she didn't seem too phased.

"I had fun. So don't worry."

"You had fun?"

"Yeah." She nodded. "You're fun." It was a simple compliment, but it meant a lot to me.

"Thank you. You're fun too." The ride back was pretty quiet after that, but it wasn't awkward. It had just been a long day, and it felt like we were just both being thoughtful.

I dropped Callie off at home and headed back to my place. It was the end of my investigation, and I was a little sad about that fact. It was time for me to trust it all to Isaak... or whatever.

Chapter Twelve

The next morning, I woke up and rolled to my side so I could look over at Pyrus on her doggie bed. She must have sensed my eyes on her because she turned to me.

"You were asleep when I got home, so I didn't get to tell you what happened, but it was crazy," I started. Then, I told Pyrus everything that happened from the moment I picked up Callie until I got back home. She patiently listened to me though she did seem a little bored.

"I don't think I can just leave the investigating to Isaak. I mean, sure, he seems capable or whatever, but I think he's a little limited in his viewpoint, if you know what I mean."

Pyrus knew exactly what I meant.

"Because, like, what in the world is going on? Why would someone order cookies to an address where they don't live under a fake name? They're just cookies! It shouldn't be this complicated..." And maybe I could have let the whole fake name thing go, but why would that same someone break into the bakery where said cookies were made. I highly doubt it was a cookie heist.

"This crime just keeps getting weirder and weirder..." I knew the answer was there though. It was just hiding from me.

Suddenly, I sat up.

"I need to go talk to Isaak. I can't leave things as they are." I jumped out of bed and ran around my room getting ready. The police station was usually open by then, so I wanted to get there as soon as possible. Pyrus watched as I scrambled to make myself presentable.

"Okay, let's take you out to pee and then get in the car." Once her business was done, we headed to the station. The Park Perdsor Police Station wasn't too big. We only had two full-time cops stationed in our town. Before Isaak came down, Trish was working with her father, but then he retired and for a little over a year, she was the only cop in town. During the off-season, it was less of a problem, but when the tourists came to town, Trish soon found herself overwhelmed. Since no one in town wanted to join, she appealed to the Providence PD, and they sent us Detective Wells.

I hadn't had a chance to ask Trish how they were getting along, but given that there wasn't really any gossip going around about any tension in the department, I assumed it wasn't too bad.

I went inside and easily located Isaak. There were only four desks in the office, so he was easy to spot.

"Isaak!" He looked up from his computer. He didn't seem surprised to see me. I wasn't sure if that was a good or bad thing.

"Lydia. How are you?"

"Great." I plopped down into the chair by Isaak's desk, and Pyrus curled up at my feet. "I came in because I wanted to ask you some questions." He looked at me like this was the exact thing he was expecting.

"Well, I'm glad you decided to come to me instead of trying to get these answers yourself." He politely smiled. I chose to rise above the snark and sarcasm and be the bigger person.

"So, I'm curious what your current theory is on what happened to Thomas Yondle."

Isaak regarded me for a few moments before nodding. "I think that property was being used as a drug house. They were probably getting all kinds of suspicious packages there, housing their product. I think it was being used as their place of operations."

A drug house? I shook my head, fully disagreeing with his hypothesis.

"I don't think Tommy was running drugs. I think something else was going on. I don't know if it was illegal, but something about this whole situation still feels off, and that offness is not explained by Tommy being a drug dealer."

There were so many reasons for me to think that it didn't work. Georgina didn't give any evidence that Tommy was using again, while the house was strange, it didn't seem like a drug operation was being run out of there. And even if they were running this massive crime ring, how did it go so unnoticed? While drugs had popped up in Park Perdsor before, there had never been a massive bust. I was pretty sure that if there was such a surge in drug activity in Park Perdsor, someone would have said something. The people in this town could not keep a secret. Even if their lives depended on it.

"I have been—"

"And what about his tox screen? Did the results come back?"

Isaak frowned at my interruption but nodded. "Yes, his tox screen results came back."

I waited to hear what it had said, but Isaak offered me nothing.

"Well!"

He gave me another annoyed look before answering. "There was nothing in his system. At least nothing that we typically test for."

"So, that supports my theory, right? If there were no drugs in his system, he wasn't around drugs!" This meant Isaak was going to start taking my ideas more seriously. He'd have to.

"That's not necessarily what the test means." Or maybe he wouldn't... "All it meant is that he hadn't used any drugs recently. Maybe he had a drug screening coming up or maybe he just wasn't using. It doesn't mean he wasn't dealing."

What? Did Isaak not understand the immense struggle an addict like Tommy would be going through being around all those drugs like that. Especially because he was newly clean and sober. If he really was committed to staying clean, he wouldn't have jeopardized his chances like that.

"Isaak, I don't think you understand—"

"No, Lydia I don't think *you* understand. I'm glad you came to me this time instead of running off and doing your own investigation, but I need you to really listen to me this time. I am taking care of this case. I will continue to take care of this case. In fact, I have some really good leads."

"Like what?" I pouted.

"Well, the owner of that house does not want to be found. It's just a trail of holding companies, but I know that eventually it will lead back to a name, and that name will hopefully lead me to a suspect."

I hated to admit it, but Isaak was right about the owner of the house being a good lead. I knew he was going to be forthcoming with any details given last night's fiasco, but I did have an idea of who could help.

"Okay, then. I'll leave you to your 'investigating'." I took Pyrus's leash and marched out of the police station. Even though I wasn't able to convince Isaak to come to my side of things, I did have a good idea on where to go next.

"He's usually at Sal's around this time." I looked down at Pyrus. "Are ya hungry?"

I walked into one of the many buildings on Main Street and came across just the man I was looking for.

"Lionel!" He was midbite on his usual order, a tuna melt, extra tuna. He seemed surprised to see me, but he masked it well.

"Lydia. It's good to see you again."

"Do you mind?" I pointed at the empty seat across from him. Lionel shook his head and motioned for me to sit down. Before I could ask Lionel what I had come there to ask him, Peter was at the table, ready to take my order.

"Well, well, well. I haven't seen this duo since you bought your bakery from Lionel." I knew Peter was looking for more gossip to share with his sister. It was unfortunate that Sal's had some of the best food in town. I was pretty sure if we as a community ate there less, our business wouldn't spread so quickly. And it wasn't just Peter and Polly's fault. Something about the diner atmosphere made people talkative.

I suspected it was the pie.

"Yeah, I just happened to see him here and thought it would be nice to have someone to eat lunch with."

"And I am very glad to have your company," Lionel commented. I quickly gave Peter my order, so he didn't have a reason to hang around. Once he was gone, I got to business.

"Um, Lionel, there was actually something I wanted to ask you about?"

"Oh!" There was a sudden spark in Lionel's eye that I hadn't expected. "Is it about your bakery?" At first, I was surprised that Lionel thought I had come to him with a question about the bakery, but then I realized it made sense. Why wouldn't he think that?

"No, I mean, not quite. It's actually a more general question."

"Oh, okay. What is it?"

"Well, I was wondering if there was a way to find out who owned a building. Or the history of owners?" I knew it was a strange question, but Lionel took it in stride.

"Yeah, that kind of info is public. It would be at the records office. It could also be online, but you might have to make a request, though it should be free to make the request." *The records office? Requests?* It sounded like that would take some time. I knew it was a good lead, but I didn't want to go down a rabbit hole which meant the murderer could be getting farther and farther away. I knew from my occasional viewing of *The First 48*, that those first few hours were crucial, and I was already passed the first two days. I didn't have much time to waste.

I could still put in a request and hopefully it would come through while I continued chasing other leads.

"Thank you. That was really helpful." Peter arrived with the bowl of soup I ordered for myself and the side of bacon I'd ordered for Pyrus. I thought she deserved to indulge a little given I'd been dragging her all over in pursuit of a criminal.

Lionel took a sip of his coke before asking me a question himself.

"Why did you want to know?"

"I was just curious." I shrugged. "Nothing serious." It looked like Lionel was waiting for me to say more, but he didn't ask any more questions. We ate in relative silence. He finished first and said he had to get back to work. Once I was alone, I picked up my phone and called Callie. Suspecting that the red tape of bureaucracy was going to slow things down, I already had another plan in mind.

"Hello?" It sounded like Callie was out by the lighthouse. I could hear the tell-tale wind.

"Are you free right now?"

Chapter Thirteen

"Are you worried Detective Wells will find out we're still... looking into things?"

"He can't be mad at us if we solve it, right?" There was only so mad Isaak could be if Callie and I came to him with the murderer's name and number, and that was my plan. I just needed to be a lot better at keeping my snooping under wraps. I wasn't sure how many more times Isaak would let us off the hook, and I didn't really want to test his patience.

While we drove to Georgina's I had Callie put in a request for documents pertaining to the abandoned house. The site said it could take up to three months to hear back which was the kind of time we did not have, but it was a good base to have covered.

Callie was able to find some documentation online, but like Isaak said, the house was owned by some random company which wasn't super helpful.

"It's called Titan Holdings, Inc, and there's nothing about it online," Callie informed me. We didn't have the long arm of the law like Isaak, so there were fewer tools at our disposal.

But that only motivated me more.

We finally pulled up to Georgina's home. I had another box of cookies to give to her. The three of us headed to the porch. I had already told Callie everything that had happened last time I was here.

Jimmy had yet to call Isaak back. Since he was out of state, it was harder for Isaak to get to him. I suspected that Jimmy was reluctant to talk to cops which was something I had on my side, but I didn't have his contact info, and I couldn't ask Isaak, so the next option was to ask Georgina, but I also didn't have her number—another thing I couldn't ask Isaak for.

Plus, I wanted to see how she was doing. I knew we weren't friends or anything, but I felt for her. I knew how hard it was to lose someone.

I went to knock on the door and saw it was already open.

"That's strange," I mumbled.

"What?" Callie asked. I motioned for her to be quieter because it didn't just look like the door was just open. It looked like someone had forced it open.

"Something's not right," I whispered. I didn't have anything to protect myself with, but I couldn't just leave in case Georgina was in danger. I looked around the porch and saw a shovel. I picked it up, holding it like a weapon.

"Lydia, what—"

"Stay out here, I'm going to see what's going on." Before I could go inside, Callie stopped me by grabbing my arm.

"I'm not letting you go in there by yourself." She did her own quick search on the porch and picked up a broom. We looked a little ridiculous with our makeshift weapons, but we were also ready to defend ourselves.

"Ready?" I asked, and Callie nodded. I pushed open the door and Pyrus immediately ran inside. We followed her into the kitchen where we found Georgina lying on the floor. It was clear someone had really hurt her.

Pyrus's barking distracted me. She was at the backdoor, sounding like she was trying to get my attention.

"You take care of her. I'm going to see what—" I didn't have to finish. Callie understood. I went with Pyrus into the backyard and saw someone running away.

"Hey!" They didn't stop. I squeezed that shovel handle, debating if it was a good idea to go after whoever it was. It was probably the same person who had murdered Tommy. Could I just let them get away? Someone who would kill and attack people like that?

I realized I barely had a choice, because what exactly was I going to do? They would probably hurt me too. Or maybe they had a real weapon. Reluctantly, I went back inside. I knew this wasn't the last time I'd have that coward in my sights.

When I went into the kitchen, Callie had Georgina's head resting in her lap.

"How is she?"

"She's in pretty bad shape. I think we have to call 911." I pulled out my phone and dialed. I gave the operator all the necessary information. I got crazy déjà vu. It was just a few days ago I'd made a similar call. I knew Isaak would have something to say about finding me in some mess again, but maybe it was destiny. What if Callie and I hadn't shown up? This murderer could have taken out an entire family, because that was what Georgina and Tommy were. A family.

"Georgina? Can you hear me?" She moaned. I knew she was in a lot of pain, but it was a good sign that she was conscious and could hear me. "Georgina. It's me, Lydia. We met a couple days ago. I called for an ambulance. You're going to get help soon. You're going to be okay, I promise." I held her hand in both of mine, giving it a squeeze.

"Lydia, I—"

"We can talk later. Save your energy, okay?" Georgina relaxed in Callie's lap. Moments later, Pyrus walked up to us with something in her mouth. "What do you have there, girl?"

She didn't stop by me, instead walking over to Callie and dropping the object by her hand. It was out of my sight, so I asked Callie.

"What is it?" She picked it up, looking down into her hand.

"It's a candy wrapper…"

"Oh no! Does it look like Pyrus ate it?" I called her over and looked into her mouth. I didn't see any evidence that she had eaten any candy.

"No, I think she just found an empty wrapper." That reassured me a little bit. If my dog got sick as well today, I wasn't sure I'd be able to handle it.

"I wonder why she brought that to you?" Maybe she was hungry, but Pyrus didn't pick food off the ground. I'd trained her pretty well in that regard. It could have been the stress getting to her. I petted her head, hoping it would help to calm her down.

I noticed that Callie shoved the wrapper into her pocket. I thought it was a little strange, but we were all under a lot of stress, and it wasn't like she'd done anything egregious. Maybe she didn't want to leave trash lying around someone else's home. There were more pressing matters to worry about anyway.

Callie and I stayed in the same position, holding onto Georgina until the paramedics came.

Chapter Fourteen

Callie and I rode with Georgina to the hospital. The paramedics were able to help her a little bit with some of the painkillers they had in the ambulance. They also set her arm because apparently the bastard that attacked her had broken it.

The closer we got to the hospital, the angrier I got. I wondered if I made the right choice by not going after Georgina's assailant. Maybe I could have taken them. I did have a shovel... and even if I had backed down, I would have seen them. I could have made an ID.

"We're here!" Callie yelled frantically. The EMTs got Georgina out of the ambulance and rolled her into the emergency room. The doctors quickly took her away, behind doors that we weren't allowed to follow her through.

Callie and I stood, staring after her. The doctors hadn't given us any information about where they were taking her or what they were going to do with her.

It made me anxious.

It didn't help my nerves when Isaak suddenly appeared.

"Crap..."

"You don't respect me, do you?" He was looking at me like a disappointed dad. Callie leaned over, so only I would hear what she had to say.

"Looks like he's mad at us." He did in fact look pissed.

"I'm sorry, Isaak. We were only—" He held up his hand to stop me from talking, and I promptly shut up.

"Yes, I am a little upset, but if you hadn't been there, *snooping*, Georgina may have been found in a much worse state." I had already had the same thought, but hearing it from Isaak made it really stick in my mind.

"Yeah..." I got some comfort knowing that my overabundance of curiosity potentially saved someone's life.

"I think maybe we should start working together. Clearly, my warnings and threats have not worked on you, and you have proven to be fairly capable. Also, I'd rather be in the know about the crazy things you are doing. The number of... phone calls I've gotten about what you've been doing."

"People have been calling you about me?"

"More like I get a call about an event, and then I arrive, and you happen to be there." I smiled at Isaak's tone. I could understand his annoyance about getting constantly shown up by a non-detective.

"Okay, okay. I'll work *with* you, but that means you really have to work with me. Promise?"

"'Promise." And he sounded quite sincere. "Now, tell me about the scene." I gave Isaak every detail I could remember about when Callie and I got to Georgina's house. When I got to the part about the assailant still being there, he was pretty excited, but that excitement died down when I revealed I didn't get a good look at them.

He also asked Callie some questions, but she was pretty out of it.

"Hey, are you okay?" Callie nodded.

"I think I'm just tired. I should probably head home." That's when I remembered I left my car back at Georgina's. I wasn't quite ready to leave Georgina yet, though. I wanted to check to see if she was okay.

"I can arrange a ride back to Park Perdsor for Callie," Isaak offered.

"Thank you." They went off, and soon Callie left. We said a quick goodbye and told her to call me if she needed anything. While Isaak and I waited for the doctors to let us see Georgina, we talked about the investigation.

"I am starting to come around to your theory that Tommy's death is not drug-related."

"Really?" I smiled.

Isaak rolled his eyes but nodded. "Yes, really. I haven't completely abandoned my theory, but with the negative tox screen and this attack of Georgina... I don't know. There could be something else going on. Maybe. Just maybe." He was finally coming over to my side. It took him some time, but I knew eventually Isaak would see that I was on the right side.

We broke down various possibilities, but there were still so many blank spots, and it was making it hard to see the forest through the trees. The who and the why of it all continued to escape us.

"Miss Hewitt. Detective Wells." Isaak and I looked up, and Georgina's doctor was standing before us. We both stood up, waiting to hear the news. "Miss Hayes is awake if you'd like to talk to her now." We both rushed to her room. She was bandaged up, but she looked much better. It put my heart at ease.

"How are you doing? How are you feeling?"

"A lot better. Thank you...for being there."

"We got lucky." I shrugged. "I brought you some cookies, but I think the box is somewhere on your porch." I wasn't sure exactly where I put it, but I knew it was not at the hospital with me. Georgina chuckled and then groaned in pain. "Sorry."

"No, the laughter is worth a little pain. It's been hard feeling happy these past few days." I took Georgina's hand in mine, letting her know I was there for her.

"I was wondering if there was anything you could tell us about the person who attacked you."

Georgina shook her head. "I barely remember it. Someone knocked on my door, and I went to answer it. Before I even really knew what was happening, he'd barged it."

"So, it was a man?"

"I think so. I wish I could tell you more." Georgina looked so upset with herself.

"You've done amazing. Don't beat yourself up. We're gonna find the man who did this to you."

She smiled at me, but it was a sad one. I decided to tell her about Tommy's tox screen because I knew she was still unsure about what led to his death. I wasn't sure if knowing about it would make her feel better, but I thought it was worth a try.

"Um, I don't know if this is helpful for you to know, but Tommy's tox screen came back clean. He wasn't on anything when he died." I made a mental note to apologize to Isaak for making the unilateral decision to tell Georgina about the tox screen later.

"So, he wasn't—"

"We don't think his death is drug-related. We're still not sure exactly what's going on, but we're going to find out."

Tears started falling onto Georgina's cheeks. "Thank you. I don't... I don't know if it makes me feel a lot better, but to know that Tommy wasn't lying to me. It helps." She let go of my hand to wipe away her tears.

"Um, could I ask you something else?"

"Sure."

"We've been having a hard time getting a hold of Jimmy. Do you think you could help us with that?"

"Oh, yeah, I should have told you he doesn't like talking to cops." Her eyes cut to Isaak.

"Why don't you send him my way. I'm not a cop!"

Georgina agreed to help us get into contact with the man. I thanked her and left my number with her in case she needed anything else.

"Oh, wait, I forgot to mention that Tommy had deposited a check from his job at one point. He usually got paid in cash, but... I don't know. The last time he got paid, it was a check."

I turned to Isaak to see if this was good news, and the look on his face told me it was.

"We could track that check to an account, get the account number and name of the holder. This is good." He smiled.

I thanked Georgina, and as Isaak and I left the hospital, I had a new pep in my step. Things were finally coming together. Every day we were getting closer and closer to catching this guy.

"You need a ride back to your car, right?"

"Um, well, yeah. I'd really appreciate it."

"Great, I'll take you." I followed Isaak back to his car. As I walked behind him, I thought about how things had... progressed between us. I wouldn't say he had fully been stripped of the "annoying" label, but things were looking up for him as well.

Chapter Fifteen

After Isaak dropped me off at my car, I followed him back to the station. On the ride back to Park Perdsor, I told Pyrus all of the thoughts I was having. She hadn't been allowed in the hospital, and so Isaak had found an officer to watch her while we waited to speak with Georgina, so I had to catch Pyrus up on everything that had happened inside the hospital.

"You were there for the drive. I feel like things have shifted between me and Isaak, but I don't know if it really means anything. Do I want it to mean anything?" I was overthinking things again. It wasn't like Isaak had professed his feelings for me. We were just being friendlier with one another. Warming up to each other as people often do.

"It's not a big deal." I shrugged. "It's not a big deal." And it wasn't. We had more important things to worry about and focus on.

When we arrived at the police station, I followed Isaak inside. Trish was there when we arrived, and she jumped up ready to leave as Isaak and I headed to his desk.

"Do you need anything before I go?" I could tell from the way she was putting on her jacket and grabbing her bag that she was hoping for and expecting a resounding no from Isaak.

And he delivered.

With confirmation that she was done for the night, Trish swiftly left, leaving Isaak and I alone to look into the new information provided by Georgina.

"So, can you just look up who wrote the check on your computer?" I pulled up a chair and sat beside Isaak and he turned on his desktop.

"Well, I don't even have to do that because Georgina sent me a copy of the check, but it isn't from a person, it's from a company, so I'm going to start digging to see if I can connect the owner of the house to whoever wrote this check and find an actual name or person connected to these 'companies'."

"Mmhm." I nodded. I watched as Isaak went to different databases and started doing different searches.

"I probably won't find the answer tonight because I have to make a records request, but I can get the ball rolling."

"Do they go faster for you? The requests?"

"Uh, yeah. Because I'm law enforcement, my requests get expedited."

That was good to hear. I wasn't sure this whole thing could wait up to a month.

I sat back and let Isaak do his thing. Suddenly, my phone rang. I checked to see who was calling, but it was a number I did not recognize.

"Do you mind if I...?"

"No, go ahead." I answered the call, bringing the phone up to my ear. "Hello?"

"Uh, my name is Jimmy. Jimmy Tate. Georgina told me to call."

"Oh my goodness, Jimmy!" I was so excited to hear from him that I jumped out of my chair. Isaak was shocked with my reaction, but he kept his cool. I thanked Jimmy for calling and gave him a quick explanation of everything that had happened. Georgina had already told him of Tommy's death, so thankfully I didn't have to deliver that news.

"So, we've just been having some trouble figuring out what Tommy was doing in Park Perdsor. We're pretty sure he was coming down for his new job, but Georgina had no idea what it could be, and there wasn't much of a paper trail. I was hoping he may have told you something about what he was doing?" I crossed my fingers hoping Jimmy would have *something* we could use.

"Uh, we did just start kinda talking. Tommy told me he was clean. That he had a new job. Wouldn't go into too many details, but he said it had to do with renovating or something." Renovations? That could explain why he was in that house. Maybe I was wrong. It still felt suspicious that there were no tools or paint or anything like that, but maybe that could be explained away.

"Did he tell you anything else?"

"No, not really. Sorry I couldn't be more helpful."

I let Jimmy know he was plenty helpful and urged him to call me if he remembered anything else before hanging up. I told Isaak everything that Jimmy told me. It wasn't a lot, but it was something to work with.

"What did Jimmy sound like? Did he seem to be telling the truth?"

'I think so." I shrugged. "Maybe a little nervous, but it didn't sound like he was lying." I did wonder if he was hiding something, but I was worried about being too pushy. I felt it was better to let him come to me.

"Okay. Hopefully we can work this renovation angle. I'm sure you'll figure something out."

"Yeah, maybe..." I answered. I wasn't so sure, but I'd try my best. Maybe talking things over with Callie would help. She should have been home by then. I got up and let Isaak know I'd talk with him later. I drove to Callie's house and knocked on her door, excited to talk about some of the information Isaak and I had uncovered.

"Lydia, hi..." Callie only opened the door enough to poke her head out. I thought it was strange, but I also knew it had been a long day, so I didn't look too much into it.

"Hey, Callie. I was wondering if you were free to talk. I was just at the police station, and we actually found out some interesting things." I sensed a nervous energy around Callie. I realized I probably should have called first, but I was so eager to talk things out with her. We made such a dream team!

But I should have slowed down and remembered that we'd had an extremely long day. And we'd been having a lot of long days, and long nights. She probably needed a moment to rest and collect herself.

"You know what, we can talk about it another day. Have a good night."

"Okay, I'll talk to you later." Callie quickly closed her door. I felt like such a jerk for not being more thoughtful.

"Come on, Pyrus." I walked Pyrus back to the car and headed home. I promised myself I would find some way to make it up to Callie. I promised her I would be an understanding and thoughtful boss, and I intended on keeping that promise.

Chapter Sixteen

The next morning, I sent a text to Callie, apologizing for going to her home uninvited. In the text, I explained how I was overly excited by the different pieces of this complicated puzzle Isaak and I had gathered, and I wanted to share it all with her, but I should have been more sensitive to the fact that it had been a very difficult day for her.

Usually, Callie would text me back pretty quickly, but when I didn't get a reply after ten minutes, I decided to start my morning routine. She would answer me when she was ready. I did all of my usual activities until I was leaning against my kitchen counter drinking my morning coffee.

That was when my phone finally pinged. I picked it up and saw a text from Callie.

No worries. I was tired last night. See u at bakery later. We can talk about it there.

Getting that text made me feel a lot better though it was rather short, and I did feel like Callie wasn't telling me everything that was wrong. That didn't mean we couldn't talk about it later if we needed to.

Once I was done with my coffee, I gathered my things, and Pyrus and I headed to work. Today was kicking off a little later than normal. There was no reason for any of us to be in super early. It wasn't like the bakery was open yet. We were just doing prep work, so I thought going in around noon was good.

The grand opening was originally scheduled for today, but I had to push it back a little given the... circumstances.

The cleaning crew came through, so I wanted to give it a few more days before we started letting customers in.

Honestly, though, even with everything going on, *Pyrus's Pastries* was in pretty good shape. While Trish wasn't able to find any extra money in the town's budget to help me with the repair and cleaning costs, she did push the paperwork through with my insurance company, so I didn't have to wait too long to get a check to cover costs. Bureaucratic red tape was so much easier to navigate with a government official on my side.

The window still needed to be repaired. There was a temporary cover while we waited on the necessary materials, but the handyman taking care of it told me they should be here in the next day or two, and that was the last thing on my list. Callie and I were going to start prepping so that by opening day, we had a decent stock of treats.

I tried not to get too excited because every time I thought I was over the hill, something else happened that threw all of my plans out of whack. I was trying an approach where I was being cautiously optimistic. I was hoping that this way I wouldn't tempt the universe into messing with my life again.

"We're just going to take it day by day, Pyrus."

Pyrus barked in agreement. We'd already talked about the plans for this week, so she was well aware of what I was thinking about. I had to keep her abreast so that there were no surprises.

As I drove, a call came in that I answered through my car's system.

"Hello?"

"Lydia! It's Georgina."

"Georgina! Hi! How are you?"

"I just got home. They discharged me this morning. My injuries looked worse than they were, thankfully, so my doctor is pretty sure I'll be able to recover at home." That was good to hear. She was in pretty bad shape when we found her, so getting the news that she was recovering well made me feel a lot better.

"Please let me know if you need anything. I'll do my best to help you out."

"I'm actually calling because I think I have some information that might help you. I plan on calling that detective Isaak, but I wanted to call you first." I wondered if she started remembering the attack from yesterday. I didn't know much about amnesia, just what I'd seen on TV. I knew it probably wasn't the most accurate representation of the condition, but people seemed to gain back bits and pieces as they reacclimated to their environment and routines.

To me, it made sense that going home would help Georgina piece together the puzzle of her memory.

"What is it? What did you want to tell me?"

"It's two things. Jimmy called me this morning. He left out some stuff when he spoke with you, and he felt kinda bad about it. He and Tommy, they've never been great with cops, and it seems to have extended to you..."

I was hoping that wouldn't be the case, but I suspected. I'd never know what it was like to be in and out of jail, but I could somewhat sympathize. I was more grateful that he was having Georgina relay the important information. It showed me he cared about his friend and wanted to get him justice.

"What did he tell you?"

"Tommy had called him the day before he died and told Jimmy he was planning on quitting his job. Something to do with his boss. Tommy wasn't giving Jimmy names or anything, but they'd actually been talking quite a bit. Tommy's new job started simple with running deliveries, letters, but then things got hairier. He didn't tell Jimmy everything, but Jimmy gathered there may have been some break-ins, destruction of property."

Like the break-in at the bakery. So, there was a series of them? Isaak never mentioned any other ones, but maybe he didn't think they were related?

"Did he say anything else?"

"Apparently, Tommy's boss was blackmailing him into continuing, but he'd had enough and planned on quitting."

So, there was the motive! Maybe Tommy even threatened to go to the police or tell other people what his boss was doing. It supported the theory that whoever owned that home or gave him that check was the one who killed him.

"You were right. That was really helpful. And the check you sent us, we weren't able to get a name just yet, but Isaak is looking into it. I can feel we're getting close."

There was something so satisfying about closing in on a suspect. Yes, we didn't have a list of possibilities, but that was fine because I felt like it was very obviously whoever hired Tommy. We just needed to get to the end of this paper trail.

The one thing that gave me pause was the possibility that whoever killed Tommy was someone from Park Perdsor. It wasn't that I thought our little town wasn't capable of violence, but whenever something like this happened so close to home... it just made me think.

"There was a second thing, right?"

"Oh yeah. Um, I'm starting to remember what happened yesterday. I'm still having a hard time remembering what the guy looked like, but there was this smell. I know this is going to sound weird, but he smelled like tuna."

"Tuna?"

"Yeah. His breath. Maybe he'd eaten something? I don't know, but it's coming back so strong. Tuna." Georgina chuckled.

Tuna... So many people ate tuna, but this person...

Was it possible? Did it really make sense? I needed to talk this over with someone just to make sure I wasn't pulling connections out of thin air because separately, what connected him to the crime, it was so... amorphous.

But put together—

"Georgina, thank you so much for telling me this! I'll let you know if we uncover anything."

I hung up the phone as I pulled up to the bakery. Maybe I could talk to Callie about what I was thinking. She might be able to help me organize my thoughts before I presented them to Isaak.

Chapter Seventeen

When I got to the door, I noticed the door was already unlocked meaning Callie was already there. I walked inside and called her name.

"Callie!"

"Yeah?" I could tell she was somewhere in the back. I was excited to get my theory out that I just started talking while I got things situated up front.

"So, I just got off the phone with Georgina, and she told me all this stuff, and I think I'm starting to piece this whole thing together." I relayed everything that Georgina had told me and what she had missed at the hospital. I told her about Tommy's job and his falling out with his boss, the check, and Isaak's attempts to connect it to whoever owned the house, and I told her about Georgina smelling tuna.

"Maybe it doesn't mean anything, but..." I paused for a second as I ran through it all in my head again. "Do you remember Lionel? We met him that day at the diner. He does a lot of development, and Jimmy said that Tommy was working in renovations or something like that which would make sense that he'd work with Lionel, right? I still haven't figured out how they would have met, but there's something there, I think."

I wasn't particularly close with Lionel or close with people who were close with him. I knew he did some travelling, so maybe he ran into Tommy at some point. I did know that Lionel was not from Park Perdsor, so it was also possible he had known Tommy from before. He'd been here for years though. I was maybe three or four when he'd moved here. Local gossip said he'd moved here with someone, but she left soon after, so I didn't know much about his background... Maybe I could get Isaak to look into it and something would come up connecting Lionel to Tommy.

"And that's not it. The tuna I mentioned. Lionel almost always gets a tuna melt, extra tuna, at Sal's, and I was eating with him before we headed over to Georgina's, and guess what he was having. A tuna melt. Maybe something I said at lunch tipped him off, and he went to Georgina's." I couldn't really remember what I told him, but if he was the murderer, then Lionel would have been able to put two and two together.

"I mean, maybe it's crazy to rest this whole thing on tuna, but something in my gut is telling me that it works. I wanted to get your opinion before I went to Isaak with it, just to make sure I don't sound crazy. So what do you think?"

I waited to hear Callie's thoughts, but she didn't say anything. I then realized she hadn't said much outside of acknowledging my earlier hello. She could be pretty quiet at times, but being *this* quiet was a little strange. It felt like she may have been ignoring me.

Maybe she was actually upset about last night despite her text.

"Uh, Callie! I'm so sorry. We should've talked about last night first. Here I come, launching straight into murder talk." It really was so easy for me to be blinded by my interests. "Oh, Pyrus. Here I go again..." I looked down at my dog, but she was hyper focused on the back. She was so still, it was almost like she was a statue.

Strange.

I kneeled down and gave Pyrus a few gentle pets.

"Is everything okay, girl?" She didn't change positions and continued to look towards the back. I was beginning to get worried, but I couldn't fathom what could be going on. Callie had answered me earlier, so I knew she was back there, and she hadn't sounded in distress in any way.

I stood back up and decided to check on Callie.

"Callie! I'm coming back there. Just wanna see if you're okay." I was about to head to the kitchen when Callie came around the corner. She stood in the entryway, a strained smile on her face.

"Lydia. Sorry for not answering. I was... I was a little lost in thought." She seemed off, but I'd expected that somewhat. I took a deep breath and geared myself up to apologize.

"I want to say sorry for not realizing that this has probably been really tough for you, and I keep dragging you along on all these detective quests, and that isn't anywhere in your job description." She had seemed happy to accompany me on these crazy missions, but I should have reminded myself that I was her boss, and maybe she was just doing it to appease me.

"No, no. It's not that. I'm not... I'm not upset with you."

"You aren't? Is there something else going on?" I took a step forward, and Callie quickly shook her head.

"No, everything's fine. You said you had a theory about Lionel?"

"Mm-hmm." I nodded suspiciously. I repeated everything I had just said, outlining why I felt that Lionel Turner was a pretty viable suspect. Callie nodded her head, listening to everything I had to say. Though, I wasn't sure she was *really* listening. She seemed somewhat distracted. I noticed her eyes darting to the back a few times.

"Callie, are you okay? Like, really okay?"

"I'm fine. I said I was fine." She shrugged. "Are you going to Isaak with this theory right now?"

"Um, maybe? It's a little haphazard right now, but—"

"Well, why don't we wait until it's less haphazard, huh? We can do some more investigating on our own and then go to Isaak together with a better idea of what happened."

I saw Callie glance backwards again, and at that point, I knew something was not right. Was there someone else here? I couldn't think of a person Callie could bring to the bakery that I would be upset about. If she wanted to show a friend around, I was perfectly fine with it.

What was she hiding?

"Callie, let's go talk in the kitchen." I tried to walk to the back, but Callie grabbed my arms and stopped me.

"Lydia, you can't!"

"Callie, what is it?" There was clear panic in Callie's eyes. I lowered my voice so only she could hear me. "Is there someone else back there?" I could feel Callie shaking as she looked at me. I waited for her to tell me what in the world was going on, but before she could answer, another voice oozed out from the kitchen.

"Lydia, Lydia, Lydia. You are just too smart for your own good." I recognized that voice. I looked at Callie with a question in my eyes, but she didn't need to answer it because the person behind the voice came strolling out moments later.

"Lionel."

Callie spun around, coming to stand by my side. At the same time, before I could stop her, Pyrus ran off and disappeared. I wasn't sure where she went. I just hoped she found somewhere to be safe.

Callie's grip on my arm tightened. This finally explained why she'd been so nervous. Lionel must have been holding her hostage in the back waiting for me to arrive.

But how did he know I'd suspected him? Sure, he'd have heard my theory while I was talking earlier, but there had to be a reason why he came here in the first place. There was no way he'd have known what Georgina told me while I was in the car. So why was he at my bakery?

"What are you doing here?" I asked, wanting an answer. Had he followed me? Bugged me? There was no way Lionel was that much ahead of everything.

However, instead of answering my question, Lionel pulled a gun out, pointing it at me and Callie.

"I'll be asking the questions from here on out."

Oh my goodness. This was starting to become quite the pickle. To put it mildly…

Chapter Eighteen

"Callie, come here." Lionel beckoned Callie over. This time I held onto her with dear life. I wasn't about to let him hurt her.

"Listen, Lionel. I am not about to let you hurt her. Your issue is with me and—"

"What are you talking about?" Lionel looked fully confused. How could he be confused? He was the one threatening us with a gun! The situation seemed pretty clear-cut from my end.

I wasn't sure what to say to Lionel in that situation. As I searched for the words, a sudden understanding came across his face, and he smiled at me. I didn't like the way his smile looked. It was like he knew something I didn't. Callie pulled on my arm.

"Lydia, there's something—"

"No, wait, Callie. Maybe she'll figure it out on her own." That was when I realized whatever was going on, Callie was already privy to it. I turned to her, trying to see if I could read her face and figure out what in the world was going on.

I looked between the two of them, and the only conclusion I was able to come to was that they were working together. That could explain why Callie was so eager to investigate with me. She was probably reporting everything back to Lionel.

I pulled myself out of her grasp and took a couple steps back.

"Ah, ah. Not too far now."

"Are you two working together?"

Lionel tilted his head to the side and shrugged while Callie looked away from me.

"You could say that. I was the one who told Callie to apply here. I wanted to keep an eye on you." Why would Lionel want to keep an eye on me? Callie and I had started talking long before we found Tommy's body, so Lionel wouldn't have sent her to keep track of the investigation.

There had to be another reason. I thought through my recent interactions with Lionel. When he sold me the bakery, everything went pretty smoothly. It was actually a quick transaction. About a month later, Lionel did come back to me asking if I'd be interested in selling the property back to him. He even offered me a different spot, but I refused because I'd already put in some work and switching spots just seemed like it would be too difficult.

Lionel never brought it up again, so I just let it drop. I never asked Lionel why he wanted to buy back the bakery. It wasn't that I wasn't curious or nosy or any of my typical personality traits, but I had been so busy trying to figure out my own overwhelming life, Lionel's just wasn't top of my list of things to delve into.

But maybe that was it. It all came back to the bakery. The building.

"Is this because I wouldn't sell this place back to you?" Lionel didn't say anything, but Callie nodded.

"He wants the land back because—"

"Callie!" She immediately froze up. Lionel saw the fear on her face, and he looked a little... guilty about it. He walked over to her and took her hand. He spoke to her in hushed tones, but the bakery was so quiet, I could still hear what they were saying.

"You don't need to tell her anything, okay."

"Yeah, but—"

"I'll take care of everything. I know things have gotten a little crazier than you expected, but I will take care of it all. We'll finish up here, and then we can go somewhere else and start over."

"Why can't we just leave now?" Lionel didn't say anything, just raised his other hand and stroked the side of Callie's head. She seemed to understand what he meant without him talking. "Okay, Dad," she sighed. *Dad?*

"Lionel is your father?" They both turned towards me. Callie looked particularly guilty at my revelation, but Lionel didn't seem to care too much that I'd figured it out. In fact, it seemed like he wanted me to know.

"Yes, Callie is my daughter. We've recently reconnected, and we are going to continue to foster our relationship once you are out of the way." *Out of the way?* Was Lionel planning on killing me? I really didn't want to die. Not like that.

"Please don't hurt her. She hasn't done anything, and she's been really nice to me. And maybe if we go to the police—"

"Go to the police!" Lionel shouted. "Why would I do that?" Lionel's attention was back on Callie, and I felt like I could use this as an opportunity to escape. Knowing that Callie was Lionel's daughter gave me some hope that he wouldn't hurt her. Not like he would hurt me. I could go and find help. I still wasn't fully aware of what Callie's full involvement was with this whole affair, but I doubted she'd helped Lionel destroy property and kill people. It seemed like she got wrapped up in her father's schemes.

I started inching to the side away from Lionel. It was a good thing Pyrus had already left, so I didn't have to worry about her wellbeing as well.

I headed towards the backdoor. The backyard was fenced in, but there was a door I could use or there were paths to climb over the fence. My gaze went between my exit and the arguing duo. It was more Lionel yelling and

Callie trying to calm him down, though. I could tell Callie had seen me, but she didn't say anything. She continued talking to her father.

"I don't know what happened that night with Tommy, but if you turn yourself in, they'll be more lenient." Callie kept pleading with Lionel, but he wasn't going to come around to her way of thinking.

"I can't go to jail. I thought you wanted to spend more time together. How much time can we spend together if I'm locked up?"

If I wasn't running for my life, I'd tell Callie not to let a jerk like Lionel manipulate her, but it wasn't the time or the place.

I was just a few feet away from the back door when Lionel turned his gun on me. His eyes weren't far behind. If looks could kill, I would have been dead on the spot.

"Where do you think you're going?"

"Oh, um..."

"Callie. Tie her up." His voice sent a chill through me. Lionel was clearly losing his patience. I didn't know what his plan was, but time was probably running out for him which meant he'd be getting more desperate.

"You know what. I can just sit down. I won't try to—"

"Tie her up!"

Callie ran to get something to restrain me with. She found some zip ties and then guided me to a chair. While she tightened the zip tie on my wrists, she leant close to my ear. "I'll figure something out. I promise," she whispered. Callie didn't fully tighten the restraint, leaving some room for me. I could probably get out of them if I needed to. The chair faced Lionel, so I was able to hide my wrists from him. Keeping my movements as minimal as possible, I started trying to get the zip tie off.

"Is she tied up?" Callie nodded. "Okay, we'll need money. We can take your car and switch out at some point." Sounded like Lionel was planning on going on the run and taking Callie with him. She didn't seem on board with the idea but barely protested.

He took Callie aside and whispered so that I could not hear what they were saying. Once the planning was done, Lionel motioned to me. Callie shook her head, but he pushed his gun into her hands.

"I don't want to..." Lionel placed his hands on Callie's shoulders and guided her towards me.

"Callie, do this, and we can leave without anything holding us back. She's seen too much. She'll tell the police what she's seen. This way, they'll be slowed down at least." Callie held the gun in her hands, looking down at it.

Even though I had faith in her, I was worried that the stress of the situation might cause her to make the... wrong choice.

"Listen, Callie. You don't have to do this. I know if we go to Isaak, he'll listen to you. He won't blame you—"

"And what about me?" Lionel asked. "She wants you to leave me rot. To abandon your own family."

Ugh! I had never been friends with Lionel, but I never knew he was so sleazy. He was such a horrible person. I couldn't believe someone like him had a daughter as sweet as Callie, and there he was, pushing her to be a bad person.

"True family would never make you do something like this. Never!" Callie's hand gripped the gun. My heart pounded faster and faster as I waited for her to make a choice. Callie started to raise the gun. She was still facing me, so the barrel was getting higher and higher on my body. I held my breath, closing my eyes.

"But... didn't you abandon me?" I didn't think that question was directed at me, so I opened one eye to see what was happening and saw Callie's back. She had the gun pointed at Lionel. His hands were raised in surrender as he stared at his daughter.

"What are you talking about, Callie?"

"I know my mother left you, but you never wrote. You never called. After the separation, we spent so little time together."

I went back to trying to break my restraints while Callie confronted Lionel.

"You know your mother kept you away from me. She was so upset—"

"That's just a bad excuse that absentee fathers use to make themselves feel better about their bad choices. If you wanted to be a good father, you would have been a good father." The end of the gun was shaking ever so slightly. Callie must have been a nervous wreck. Unfortunately, I wasn't the only one who noticed.

"Despite all of that, I am still your father. And I'm trying to be a good one. You know that. Haven't these past couple months been good?" Lionel took a tentative step forward. Callie's eyes went wide as her grip on the gun tightened.

"Don't move!"

"Callie, come on." Lionel didn't listen to her command at her and kept moving closer and closer. Callie had taken a few steps back, but there was minimal room to move, and soon there was nowhere else to go

"Callie, don't listen to him. He's just saying all of that to manipulate you. If he loved you, he wouldn't treat you like this!" I hoped and prayed for my words to get through to her. Even if they didn't save me, I hoped they'd save her because if this whole debacle ended with Callie being stuck on the run with the sad sack that was Lionel, I would have to come back from the dead and haunt them until Callie came to her senses.

"No, Dad! No! You weren't there for me, and I'm done listening to you. If you take another step towards me, I will shoot you." The determination in Callie's voice told me she was not playing, but Lionel must not have been convinced because he took another step. I saw Callie's finger squeeze the trigger.

Everything seemed to slow down as I watched Callie shoot Lionel.

Chapter Nineteen

*C**lick.*
 Callie pulled the trigger back all the way, but nothing came out. She didn't have a chance to check the gun because Lionel grabbed it from her.

"Did you—"

"I wanted to see what you would do, and it looks like you'd shoot me if you had the chance!" I couldn't believe the series of events that had just transpired. From thinking that Callie was going to shoot me to thinking that Callie was going to shoot Lionel to finding out that it was all just one big crazy test conducted by Lionel to test Callie's loyalty.

The whiplash was insane.

I watched as Lionel grabbed another chair and pushed Callie into it. He tied her hands as well. It gave him a nice old view of my loosely tied hands.

"Well, that's not right." Lionel grabbed the end of the zip tie and gave it a strong pull.

"Ow!" It was so tight that I could barely move my hands. I couldn't see a way out. With Callie and I both tied up, there was no one to come and rescue us. Maybe if I'd called Isaak before walking into the bakery, we'd have a chance, but he had no clue what was going on and probably wouldn't find our bodies until much later.

Lionel walked to the other side of the kitchen and pulled out the clip he had taken out of the gun. He shoved it in and pulled back the slide. Once he was satisfied the gun was loaded, Lionel took out his phone and made a call.

I turned to Callie. Well, I turned my head towards Callie because my body was going nowhere.

"Callie?" Callie's head was hanging like she had zero strength in her neck. She looked absolutely defeated. "Callie?" She didn't turn to me, instead letting out an intelligible moan. "I just want you to know that I'm not mad at you. You tried really hard to save my life. Hell, you were willing to shoot your dad over it." Maybe she could have come to me sooner with the truth, but I understood why she hadn't. It could be hard betraying someone you believed was close to you. Even after they betrayed you.

"I'm sorry, Lydia. I didn't know my dad had killed Tommy. Not until later. I should have told you when I figured it out, but I just had to make sure before I did anything because if I was wrong..." She shook her head. I probably would have done the exact same things she did.

And that was why it was hard for me to hold a grudge.

"How did you figure out it was your dad?" Callie finally looked up at me.

Her eyes were wet with tears. "When we found Georgina, the candy wrapper that Pyrus gave me was this candy my dad's always eating. They're hard caramels. Yeah, it was small, but I started putting the other strange details together. The holding company being named Titan, him recommending I apply here.. It was too much."

"What's the deal with Titan?"

"It was his nickname for me when I was a kid," she shrugged. "Whenever we watched *Hercules*, I loved the part with the titans, and I would pretend to be them." That would have been cute if I wasn't so freaking angry with Lionel.

"That's why I didn't feel ready to tell you. I just had to make sure…" In that moment, I wished I could have reached over and comforted Callie. She really looked like she needed a hug. "Now, we're going to die," she sobbed.

I knew I was just wallowing in our abysmal situation, but we couldn't both be hopeless. I started looking around for a way for us to get out of this situation. There had to be *something*.

"We're going to get out of this, Callie. We aren't meant to die today."

"Okay," she didn't sound like she believed me, but that wasn't going to take away my hope. In that moment, I was going to be Callie's Pyrus. I was going to give her hope.

But, as it turned out, I didn't need to dig so deep because the darndest thing happened next.

"Pyrus!" My dog came running back into the bakery. I had no idea what possessed her to return to this highly dangerous scenario, and I couldn't tell if I was happy or upset to see her. Happy because she was my good girl, but upset because there was a crazy man with a gun.

"Is that your dog?" Lionel hung up his phone call when he saw Pyrus running back into the kitchen. He pointed his gun at her, and that was when he became the lowest of the low in my eyes.

"Don't you dare!" A sudden strength rose up in me, and I stood up, chair and all. Without even thinking, I bum-rushed Lionel, gun be damned, but before I could reach him, and possibly do myself grievous harm, Isaak came rushing in.

"Lydia!" The entire room turned to look at him. He too had his gun out and was pointing it at Lionel. "Drop your weapon!"

Lionel kept his gun trained on me, and I realized I was probably in the worst position to be in this stalemate. Tied to a chair, no weapon, in between two men with guns.

Crap.

Isaak could shoot Lionel, but that didn't mean Lionel wouldn't shoot me. And yes, I was being all self-sacrificing earlier, telling myself if only Callie got out of this situation, it would be okay as long as she didn't go with her dad, but my tune had changed given that there was more of a chance that I might survive.

Honestly, if it could be avoided, I did not want to die.

"If you do not back up, I will shoot her." I gave Isaak my panicked eyes. If he backed up, Callie and I would be in the same exact position, stuck with Lionel and his stupid gun, but if Isaak didn't back up, there might be the new problem of Lydia with a bullet in her body.

Quite the lose-lose for me.

"Listen, Lionel. We can talk about this. It doesn't have to end this way."

"Don't tell me how this needs to end. I'm getting out here, and you can't stop me." Lionel started walking towards me.

"What are you doing?"

"Well, if I'm going to get out of here, I'll need a hostage." *Oh hell no.* I changed my mind. I was not going to a second location with that man. I would take a non-fatal bullet. The shock would help with the pain, right? Adrenaline would keep me from feeling like I was dying.

That or I'd pass out.

"Isaak, take the shot! Isaak, take the shot!" I started yelling at him the closer Lionel got to me. I was getting desperate, but I knew there was nothing he could do. He wasn't going to get me potentially shot just because I told him to.

Ugh!

Luckily for me, there was someone we had all forgotten about in the kerfuffle.

Pyrus came running towards Lionel and bit him directly on the butt.

"Argh!" Lionel pointed his gun upwards as he tried to get Pyrus off giving Isaak the opening he needed. He shot Lionel in the leg, and the man dropped to the ground like a sack of potatoes. I quickly ran off back to where Callie was still tied up.

Isaak placed his body between us and Lionel, so Lionel couldn't use us as collateral anymore.

Somehow, the man had held onto his gun. It was sheer stubbornness at that point because there was no way he was getting out of this.

"Drop your weapon!" Isaak commanded again. Lionel moaned as blood spurted out of his leg. I looked over at Callie who had passed out. Isaak kept repeating the same command again and again, but Lionel would not let go of his weapon.

Even with a wounded leg and no chance of getting out, he raised his gun and pointed it at Isaak. Without hesitating, Isaak took the shot, and Lionel dropped to the floor again. That time, he didn't get up.

"Did you—"

"He's dead," Isaak plainly stated. "We need to get her out of here." He pointed at Callie. I agreed. Even though her and her dad had a *very* complex relationship, I knew she wouldn't want to see him like that.

I told Isaak where to grab some scissors. He cut me free and then freed Callie. I helped him carry her into the next room.

"Where are you taking me?" she mumbled, barely awake.

"Just to lie down." We brought her to one of the booths and sat her upright. "What happens now?" I asked Isaak. This was the second dead body in my bakery in a week. Was I upset? One hundred fifty percent, but I had to keep looking forward.

"The medical examiner will have to come. There will be an investigation into whether this was a justified use of deadly force," Isaak sighed.

I placed my hand on his forearm. "I'll talk to whoever you need me to talk to."

"Thank you." We looked at one another for a few beats but were interrupted by Callie jolting awake.

"Are we safe?"

I placed my hands on her shoulders to help calm her down.

"It's okay, Callie. Isaak saved us." Her eyes darted back and forth between the two of us before she threw her arms around me.

"I'm so sorry, Lydia! My dad's been terrorizing your bakery, and I've only made it worse, and if you never want to talk to me ever again, I understand. I just hope that someday—"

"Callie, Callie." I pulled my body back, so I could look Callie directly in her eyes. "I've already forgiven you, okay? Let's just try and move forward, huh?" She sniffled and nodded. Pyrus walked out from the back, stopping in front of Callie and resting her paws on Callie's knees as she stood on her hind legs.

"Here comes your real savior," Isaak said.

"What do you mean?"

"Pyrus is the one who came and got me. She would not stop barking until I followed her."

"But how did you know to come to the bakery?"

I saw Isaak's car outside, and I doubted Pyrus gave him directions.

"That was an educated guess."

I gave Pyrus a huge hug. She was literally a life saver. I couldn't believe it.

"What about my dad? What happens to him now?" Isaak and I glanced at one another before I took Callie's hands and explained what happened to her. She sat silently as I told her that her father had been shot by Isaak in order to protect the two of us. When I finished, she just looked at me blankly.

"I'd like to go home."

"Of course," Isaak answered. "I'll need to speak with you about what happened at some point. Why don't you drop by the station tomorrow, okay?"

"I'll drive you home, honey. Okay?" I told Callie to go wait in my car. I wanted to finish speaking with Isaak before we left. "So, is it just going to be a quick witness statement?" Isaak looked uncomfortable at my question. "What is it?"

"I have to question Callie about what she knows. She was clearly hiding some information from us, and I need to know how much she was hiding." I crossed my arms over my chest and gave Isaak my very cross face.

"She had nothing to do with the murder or the sabotage. Lionel was manipulating her as much as us."

"And I'm sure my inquiry will uncover that, but I still have to do it."

I knew Isaak had just saved our derrieres, but knowing he was going to interrogate Callie upset me. I too wanted to go home.

"Fine. I'll see you tomorrow." I called Pyrus to follow me and got into the car to drive Callie home. It was quiet all the way to her house.

"See you tomorrow?" I asked her as she got out.

She paused for a second before answering. "Yeah, tomorrow." She shut my door and headed into her house. Her answer wasn't convincing, but there was nothing I could do. I just hoped that wasn't the last time I'd see her.

Chapter Twenty

A few weeks later.

It had been some time since Isaak had closed the case. As I predicted, Callie didn't go with me to the station the next day. She went on her own and had a separate interview with Isaak. I had tried calling and texting, but it would appear she didn't want to talk to me.

I wasn't sure if she was mad at me, or if maybe she was mad at herself. It had been an overly awful week, and it seemed she needed a little space to get her head back on right.

My interview with Isaak went pretty smoothly. I told him everything I saw and had figured out. I also finally turned over that spare key I found, having realized it probably belonged to Lionel.

After the hostage situation and the shooting, I closed the bakery for about a week. I had the cleaners come in, but that was about it. I needed time to reorient myself and figure out what I really wanted to do. Having a near-death experience put a lot of things in perspective for me.

It made me realize that the dream I had had all my life was still the dream I wanted to pursue, but I also realized I had gotten so wrapped up in becoming a professional baker that I had let other parts of my life fall to the wayside. I started spending more time with my friends. Gage, Trish,

Peter, Polly, and I went to explore the cove together. Something I hadn't done since I was a teenager.

Gage and I also started hanging out outside of the USPS building more.

"How are things with Detective Wells?" We'd avoided *that* topic for quite a while, but I knew Gage was buzzing with curiosity. Unfortunately for him, there wasn't much to report.

"Things are fine. I haven't seen him recently. He's busy. I'm busy." I shrugged.

"Oh, I thought..."

"Nope. It was probably just the thrill of the case or whatever. Turns out, he is kind of annoying." I partially blamed him for Callie not talking to me. Maybe if he hadn't insisted on treating her like a suspect, she wouldn't have felt the need to disappear. Not to sound like a stalker, but I had driven past her house a couple times, and her car wasn't there. No one in Park Perdsor had seen her for weeks.

Maybe our little town held too many painful memories for her.

After my week of rest and relaxation, I got back to getting my bakery in shape. I took my time, not so worried about reaching some arbitrary deadline. That being said, money was starting to become a problem. It wasn't impossible for me to keep paying my mortgage, but it was financially stupid, given the bakery wasn't earning any money. It could be months, maybe years before I was able to get the place open again.

I really, really wanted to make my dream work, but it was either work myself into an early grave because I dropped dead from all the stress or give it up and try to enjoy the life I had.

Reluctantly, I listed the bakery for sale. It wasn't the hottest property, but there were a few inquiries. Almost all of them were below asking price, but there was one that came from an anonymous buyer that bid a couple thousand above what was listed. I had to call the realtor to see if it was real.

"Yeah, I was shocked myself. The buyer did have one request that it be done all through me, so they could stay anonymous..." I had no trouble honoring that request. The fact that I'd be coming out of the entire deal not in debt put me over the moon.

But as the due date for the paperwork approached, I began feeling quite sorrowful because I was losing my business. I had everything signed waiting on my dining room table. I just needed to fax it to the realtor.

"Should we say goodbye to the store, girl?" I leashed Pyrus up, and we headed to the bakery one last time. As I stood outside the storefront, I wondered what it would become. It could literally be anything. A clothing store, a bookstore. They could sell touristy tchotchkes or do bike repairs. At the end of the day, it wasn't really my concern anymore.

As I stared at what was still my bakery for the next couple hours, I felt Pyrus pulling at her leash. I turned to see where she was trying to go and saw Callie approaching us.

"Callie! What are you doing here?"

"Hey, Lydia..."

I realized my question sounded a little rude, so I rephrased it. "I meant, how are you?"

"Good. Better. I've been spending some time with my mom. It was helpful." I still didn't know a lot about Callie's mom, but I did remember she told me they had a strained relationship. It sounded like it was getting less strained, which was nice.

"That's great."

"What about you?"

"Okay. I decided to sell the bakery. It didn't make financial sense to keep it, so yeah..." I had already cried all the tears I needed to cry, so I was just basking in the good memories.

"Oh, who did you sell it to?"

"The buyer was anonymous, so I don't know, but they had the best offer."

"Yeah. Well above asking."

"What?"

"Huh?" Callie looked at me confused, but she was the one who said something weird.

"You said well above asking. How did you know it was well above asking?" Callie looked at the ground like she had something to hide "Callie?"

"Okay, okay. So, I bought the bakery…"

"You bought it!" I couldn't believe my ears. Callie was going to be the new owner of my old bakery. "Why?"

"I saw that you had listed it, and I felt bad. It was partially my fault that everything went haywire. I was my dad's next of kin which meant I suddenly had a lot more money than I knew what to deal with, so I thought this would be the best way to pay it forward, so you wouldn't have to lose what you worked so hard for. Okay!" I was shocked. Speechless. Flabbergasted. Callie Pierson had disappeared from my life only to fly back in and save my bakery.

"Callie, I don't know what to say."

"Say you'll buy it back from me!"

"Oh, well, the money you're paying for the store is going to go to the bank to finish paying the loan, and what I'll have leftover won't be nearly enough." And I was totally fine working at a bakery Callie owned. She'd make a way better owner than the bank or her father.

"Well, you don't know what my asking price is. How can you turn me down without knowing the price?"

"Okay, what's the price?"

"Mmm… $1." My eyes went wide. She could not be serious.

"Did you say 'one dollar'?"

"I think that's more than fair. Maybe you could throw in a plate of cookies?" Oh my goodness. There was no way she was being serious, but her face was telling me this wasn't a joke.

"Callie, now I really don't know what to say."

"Say you'll hire me again. I'd love to work with you again." I didn't even have to think about it. Of course I wanted to work with Callie. The entire time she was gone, I missed her terribly and kept going over in my mind what had happened. The only difference I was thinking was, that with everything we had gone through, maybe we should be partners instead.

It was an idea I thought I could bring up with her later. First, I wanted to celebrate. Not just the rebirth of my business, but also the return of a dear friend. My hero dog Pyrus would like that as much as I did.

"To Sal's!" It would be the perfect place to get the word out that *Pyrus's Pastries* was back!

About the Author

Miranda Rose Barker has enjoyed the company of dogs from the age of 7. She only later discovered the rewarding world of dog rescues in her mid-30's and since then, has lived with eight rescue dogs, including large and small mixed breeds from German shepherds to doodle dogs and some purebreds (schnauzers and other terriers).

A lifelong writer, she began writing fiction in 2000 and has loved bringing rescue dogs and their humans together in her books for years. She also delights in reading and writing cozy mysteries, usually ones with an amusing dog character.

Miranda Rose lives in southern California, where she is often out looking for the next rescue pup to add to her own pack or a friend's pack.

Check out more of Miranda Rose Barker's latest titles in her book series: *The Sycamore Grove Ghostly Cozy Mystery Series, The Tansy & Hank Pet Psychic Cozy Mystery Series, The Dog Lovers' Rescue Romance Series, The*

Very Human Dog Lover Story Series, The Near-To-Home Mystery Novels, The Sweets of Saltcaster Cozy Mystery Series, the Sweets of Snowkeep Cozy Mystery Series, The Dogs Are Family Too Series, and much more.

Visit Miranda's website to learn more about topics mentioned in the Tansy & Hank and Sycamore Grove cozy mystery series – e.g., Tarot and other ways to boost intuitive insights and Crystal Healing at https://mirandarosebarker.com

Visit Miranda Rose Barker's *Amazon Author Page* or visit https://author.to/mirandarosebarkerbooks to learn more about her books and book series...

Remember To Claim Your Free Gift

Dear Reader –

Thanks for reading my book!

Sign up for my mailing list to receive exclusive copies of some of my future books as well as to be notified of any new releases, giveaways, contests, cover reveals and so much more.

Just click below to claim your free book and newsletter updates. See you soon...

https://mirandarosebarker.com/cozy-mystery-offer

Dogs Are the Nicest People

Mysteries by the Author

Visit https://mirandarosebarker.com/mrbauthorpage

The Near-To-Home Mystery Series
Straying Home
The Prodigal Returns
The Lost Estate
Family Matters
Family Business

Cozy Mysteries by the Author
The Sycamore Grove Ghostly Cozy Mystery Series
The Ghostly Visitation
If There's A Will, There's A Ghost
The Ghostly Treasure Hunt
The Ghostly Art of Flowers
The Scandalous School Mystery
The Persnickety Apparition Mystery
The Ghostly Girl Mystery
The Apple Orchard Ghost Mystery

The Missing Ghost Mystery

The Tansy & Hank Pet Psychic Cozy Mystery Series
The Foot in the Fountain Mystery
The Crystal Conundrum
The RV Riddle
The Curse of Pine Ridge
The Christmas Cookie Caper
The Baffling B and B Mystery
The Teapot Tempest Mystery
The Murder Map Mystery
A Rash of Murders Mystery
The Shocking Chalet Mystery
The Worrisome Wedding Mystery
The Not-OK Corral Mystery

The Sweets of Saltcaster Cozy Mystery Series
Baked in Suspicion
Write and Wrong
Influenced to Death

The Sweets of Snowkeep Cozy Mystery Series
The Pumpkin Bread Mystery
The Cupcake Calamity Mystery
The Doughnut Delivery Mystery

A Little-Pinch-of-Murder Mystery Series
The Magical Bagel Mystery
Cookied: A Little-Pinch-of-Murder Mystery

Review This Book on Amazon…

Just visit the Amazon page for this book and scroll down below the *About the Author* section on the book page.

Once there, you can click the "**Review this product**" link in the left-hand column, just below existing Customer reviews.

If you run into any issues posting an Amazon review, try posting one on GoodReads.com or BookBub.com

Please share an honest review *(and, if you received an Advance Reader Copy (ARC) Team copy of the book, please say so in your Amazon review).*

Click Here to Review This Book

www.ingramcontent.com/pod-product-compliance
Lightning Source LLC
LaVergne TN
LVHW090038121224
798917LV00038B/907